Uriah's Utopia

Gloria Smit

Lost Lake Folk Art

SHIPWRECKT BOOKS PUBLISHING COMPANY

IN®
DIE

Minnesota

Cover Painting: by James David Smit
Traveling Saints (2011), acrylic on hardboard, 28"x25"

Cover and interior design by
Shipwreckt Books

For my fictitious characters. You know who you are.

Uriah's Utopia

Contents

Part 1

A Preposterous Scheme

"Uriah, I'll go with you to Promise, but I'm not guaranteeing I'll like it, or that we'll stay," I said. We drove south on I-57 and turned west at Chabanse, Illinois. "It's spooky around here. These deserted farms, one after another, it creeps me out."

"That's why Victor chose this place. There's plenty of land and there won't be much concern from the local farmers as the community grows. It's perfect—no one lives around here anymore."

"If the community doesn't have enough housing, where will we live?"

"We'll find out what's available when we get there."

"Hopefully."

"Come on, Alodie, could you be more positive about this?"

I just shook my head. The whole scheme was preposterous. Some guy, who claims to be clairvoyant, writes a book about the world coming to an end. Before the earth is inundated by rising seas and earthquakes, this group of 'special' people are to build a self-sufficient society that weathers a cataclysm and starts a new civilization. Who are these 'highly evolved and chosen'? Us?

What Victor seemed to know about Uriah convinced us to give Promise a try. We attended an introductory meeting in Chicago during the early spring of 1974. Victor gave a lecture about his connection with the Great Brotherhood and talked about the development of the new community. Uriah put up a bandaged hand to ask a question. Victor said, "You must be a wood-worker."

Uriah was certain Victor was clairvoyant by that statement alone. How could Victor have known? I was swayed by the possibility of clairvoyance. I thought it might be real because I had had a few premonitions myself, but it was Uriah's enthusiasm that finally convinced me to quit arguing and follow his lead.

I agreed there were some good ideas in Victor's book, *The Brotherhood's Promise*. Uriah was so into it. He was happier than he'd been for at least a year. He finally had a focus, something to look forward to, and even if it was crazy, it would be better to join Promise than do nothing. Not to go anywhere or do anything exciting might sink Uriah deeper into the depression that had crept up on him since we finished college.

The ghostly loneliness of the deserted farm houses, the weathered barns, the ancient apple trees, the broken cottonwoods, and the tangled windbreaks made me sad. The homesteaders who loved this land would have been sad as well to see that corporate farms took over thousands of acres and left their homes to rot in the rain and unrelenting west wind. Was it possible to resurrect one of these farms—to bring one back to life? "Uriah, look at that house, isn't it cool?"

"You want to check it out?"

"Maybe we could. No one would care, would they?"

"Have you seen a car in the last ten miles. Who would care?"

We pulled into an overgrown driveway and my imagination went wild. I would plant the garden below the barn in the cow yard. The soil would be amazing. Uriah would have to prune the trees in the orchard, the apples were scarce, small and wormy. "Uriah look, there are lily of the valley and peonies."

"I'm going to check out the barn."

"Okay. I'll see if I can get into the house."

"Be careful, the floors may be rotten."

I was able to pry open the porch door and it almost fell off its hinges. I stepped inch by inch across the porch floor to the kitchen door—it wasn't locked. Within minutes of entering the house, I had redesigned the kitchen, refinished the oak floor, chose rooms for Zea and Milo and polished a spot on the potbelly wood stove. I could live here.

"Alodie? Where are you?"

"Up here. Watch the steps."

"I love this place, Uriah."

"We've got to get going, Hon. We're supposed to be at Promise for the tour at two o'clock."

"Okay, yeah, I just want to check out the rest of the house. How was the barn?"

"Falling down. The roof is shot and the walls are leaning."

"What about the house? Do you think it's salvageable?"

"We have to go, Alodie."

I couldn't shake the idea of renovating an old farm since we made a bid on one about a year ago. I thought, because the farm had been owned by a cousin of my dad's, we would have first dibs, but the executor of the estate didn't even let us know when it was sold to someone else. Our bid was too low. We couldn't have bid higher because we didn't have any money. All of our dreams were plugged into that farm. We were going to fix up the house and the barn, and then invite our dispersed and wandering friends to join us. We would start a commune and make it a utopia.

But here we were, on our way to checking out someone else's dream, someone else's utopia, and it had all sorts of occult dogma attached to it. But hey, if Uriah was happy again, I was happy. What did we have to lose?

CR

We turned onto a paved, curbed, side-walked street in the middle of a cornfield after we saw a sign: "Welcome to Promise." The first structure that grabbed my attention was a two story, blue, mansard roofed house—totally out of place. Where are we? In a Jane Austin novel? We drove around a couple of loops until we saw a more reasonable ranch style house with a sign that read "Promise Office" and parked in front. "Is this somebody's house? Should we knock?"

Uriah knocked and then opened the door a crack. "Welcome. Welcome," a 50-ish gray-haired man in a green V-neck sweater startled us as he swung the door open wide. "Come in and join the group. We'll introduce ourselves and start the meeting in a few minutes. Grab a cup of coffee or tea. The bathroom is over there."

I was glad for a brief escape to the bathroom. We were late—my fault—and being late made me anxious. I took a couple of deep breaths while alone in the room, combed my hair, left the bathroom and grabbed Uriah's hand on the way to open seats in the back row.

The man in the green sweater, David, commenced the meeting. He introduced Victor. Uriah poked me with his elbow. Victor was the guru. He was the guy who knew what no one else was privy to and had the connection to the adepts who were giving him inside information on the fate of the planet. They had taught him skills we wanted to learn—skills like telepathy, astral travel, seeing auras, knowing our past lives and being able to use the power of attraction to better our circumstances. If these abilities were possible, Promise was the place to learn them. Victor would be our teacher.

Victor welcomed us briefly and hoped we would consider joining Promise. He said we would not have been in the room without direction from the Great Brotherhood. Then, he disappeared into a back room. I wanted to hear more from Victor—he was a mysterious man, soft spoken, but he oozed some kind of mesmerizing power.

Victor's wife, Beatrice, stood and nodded to the group. I thought she was a bit stern looking with blond hair—dyed probably and rolled into a French twist. She wore a tight over-the-knee skirt, nylons and spike heels. Was she trapped in the 1940s?

Beatrice explained the philosophy of the school. It was a combination of the philosophies of Marie Montessori and Rudolf Steiner. She explained the belief and practice at Promise that mothers stayed at home and tutored their children. A wife's role was to care for the household, including her husband. Ouch. *This,* I did not agree with.

David discussed the dress code. Women wore skirts at all times. Men were to be clean shaven with short hair. Victor and Beatrice didn't want the locals to worry about a bunch of beatniks invading the area. There goes Uriah's beard, I thought. I wore long skirts mostly anyway, with gauzy blouses, clogs or huaraches. My identity. Screw the nylons.

The president of the Promise business association, William, had a kindly smile, and gave the group a simple wave. He handed out a list of businesses and projects the community was involved in. He explained the concept of tithing. All men who joined the community were expected to tithe—to give Promise either ten percent of their work hours or income. It wasn't clear what women were supposed to give. Everything!

We followed David on a walk around Promise. He showed us the school where the older children attended for more hours a week as they were weaned from their mothers. Miss Carol, the matron of the school, had each child say 'Hello' in a different language. I was impressed.

The twenty or so houses were of a variety of types, two under construction. Uriah was curious about the power source. Everything was electric because there were nearby nuclear plants and power was cheap. Uriah had read about solar power in college and he couldn't understand why Promise wasn't experimenting with alternative energy. What about wind? There was plenty of that out here on the prairie. Uriah asked the question, but David dismissed him with a vague answer. Victor didn't want to be associated with hippie ideas of self-reliance, so I don't know what the plan was when the infrastructure was damaged or destroyed in the cataclysm the Brotherhood predicted. Maybe Victor hadn't had the time to think about that.

There were nearly two-hundred members of Promise, so where did everyone live? The visitors, who were all potential members, seemed a bit anxious about living arrangements. One little town, Cabery—almost a ghost-town, was five miles away and there were no places left to rent. The next closest towns were ten to twenty miles away and not much bigger. David said people from Promise lived all over the area including Kankakee, the nearest city, which was thirty miles to the northeast.

After the tour, we met people from as far away as New Jersey, California, and even Switzerland! It was exciting to think we might be sharing an experience with like-minded folks, mostly our age, from all over the world. We took the application forms, said good-bye, hope to see you soon, and drove to Uriah's mother's house. We were staying with her because we were in kind of a predicament.

Kind of a Predicament

Uriah and I had moved from the north side of Chicago to Champaign after finishing college because the University of Illinois was there. Uriah ended up with a bachelor's degree in psychology from Northwestern—a major he decided on because he had taken more psychology courses than any others. Uriah's aspiration in high school was to go to seminary. He dreamed of becoming a missionary in an exotic, far away land, but was disillusioned with Christianity after he mingled with friends of different persuasions. Vietnam, Watergate, and capitalism also put a dent in his idealism and messed up his plan. Art, music, and woodworking were his true loves. The University of Illinois might be an option in case Uriah decided to do graduate work, but in the meantime he needed to find a way to support his family.

I had finished my degree in nursing and could get a job anywhere. Five minutes after I walked into Mercy Hospital in Champaign's twin city, Urbana, I was snatched up with only a graduate license—my board scores weren't in yet, but it didn't matter.

Uriah tried to start a furniture business in the basement of our rented house. Marketing was tough. Rocking horses and carved coffee tables weren't in great demand. Disappointed and lonely, he looked for other work.

"Alodie," he said one day six months after moving to Champaign. "I'm going to Chicago tomorrow to interview for a job at a sheltered workshop. I can teach wood-working and maybe make some connections for my business."

I thought it was a good idea because I was six months pregnant with our second child and hoped not to have to work for a year or so after the birth.

Uriah's dad had built a cottage on the back acreage of his farm thirty miles south of Chicago. We could live there until we found a more permanent home. Uriah's dad died suddenly from a heart attack which added to Uriah's depression and confusion about who he was and what he wanted to do with his life. The cottage blew over in a tornado two months after Milo was born. Uriah quit his job when he cut his hand—a client at the workshop had turned the table saw around. Uriah had stuck his hand into the blade when he reached underneath to turn it off. Yes, we were in a predicament.

The Brotherhood's Promise had been gnawing at us. Uriah first heard about the book on a trip to Colorado at a friend's party. Then, before we left Chicago, he was handed the book by a stranger on the subway. It must have been a sign. Twice within a year, the same book had been presented to Uriah. He read it a couple of times before I got around to it. The book was intriguing and it became the main topic of our conversations.

Within a week of our visit to Promise we sent in an application and one week later we got a call from David—we had been accepted as associate members. We would have to prove our commitment to Promise before they would accept us as full members. I was okay with that because I wanted to make sure Promise was right for us too and not some kooky cultish trap.

A few days after David's call, Uriah went to Promise by himself. He found a place to live by asking around. The house was in the country about ten miles from Promise—a huge five-bedroom farmhouse. The owners, who were cash croppers, lived down the road. Uriah said the rent was reasonable, although heating it might cost us, but we could close off the upstairs. He had already signed the lease, which was fine with me, the place sounded wonderful.

CR

Uriah found a job within a week after we moved for a barn building company in the town of Herscher—fifteen miles to the east. The foreman was a member of Promise and hired men from the group. The owner liked the short-haired, clean cut men who made a practice of being good citizens. He didn't care if his employees looked like they were Mormon or Jehovah's Witness. What was that to him as long as they kept their beliefs to themselves? The construction sites could be fifty or more miles away and during the late summer and fall, Uriah worked long hours and sometimes stayed overnight. While I loved living in the country, I was glad winter came early because Uriah was home more now that construction had slowed.

Uriah was trying to teach our new Holstein calf to climb the basement steps. The lesson wasn't going well. Unless placed squarely on the tread, the calf's hard little hoofs slipped through the spaces where the risers should have been. Halfway up, neither Uriah nor the calf were sure if going up or backing down was the better option. I heard the commotion and, with dish towel in hand, approached the top step. Uriah was pushing on the calf's butt and coaxing, "Come on Mary, you can do it, Sweetie."

"Hon, why don't you just carry her up?"

"She's getting heavy and pretty soon I won't be able to lift her at all."

"Maybe by then she should move out to the barn."

"Yeah, but it's so cold out there."

"She's a cow."

"Yeah, but the kids really like playing with her."

"Yeah, but what if the landlord finds out we're raising a calf in the basement?"

Zea, who had been exploring in the root cellar, saw what her dad was trying to do and excitedly offered assistance, "I'll push too. Come on Mary Cow, come on now."

Little Milo, distracted from his inventory of pots and pans in the lower cabinet, crawled across the kitchen floor. He pulled himself up to a standing position with a strong grip on my long skirt and I steadied him with a hand on his curly blond head. "Watch out now." The calf was one step from the top.

"Good girl. You did it!" Uriah turned his attention to the kids. "Let's play outside with Mary. Get ready while I tie her."

I bundled Milo in his red snow suit and put plastic bags over his socks before slipping on his little work-boots. Zea was on her own. She was old enough to dress herself, and dressing was her passion. She added layer upon layer of clothing during the day whenever her fashion muse whispered, but if there was an assignment, the perfect article was never to be found. I handed off Milo to Uriah and went to rescue Zea. She was screaming from her bedroom closet, "Wait for me! Wait for me!"

The day before, the first winter snow had blown horizontally for hours across the prairie. The circular drive was drifted and impassable. Uriah looked across the farmyard to the empty barn and knew he would spend this Sunday afternoon shoveling snow, the same task he had completed the day before. A shift in the wind, now from the north, would sift the snow back into the tunneled drive.

The calf's lead rope wasn't necessary. Mary stayed close to Zea, too close, messing up snow angels one by one. Uriah was lobbing Milo into a snow drift and there were giggles coming from everywhere. I was content as I watched my family play.

After a Sunday brunch of banana-oatmeal pancake—Uriah's specialty, Milo went down for a nap in the oversized plywood cradle Uriah had built for Zea when she was born. Zea went to play in her imaginary world. I threw my legs over the cushy round arms of my favorite burgundy stuffed chair and embroidered a sampler that read, "Health, Love, Joy, Wealth, and the Time to Enjoy Them." Uriah dug a path through the snow from his white Chevy pickup to the plowed county road.

Irrational Adherence

The telephone rang once and stopped. I rolled over in the blue steel-framed bed and put out a hand to feel for Uriah. Up already, typical. Before I could rearrange myself comfortably, intent on falling back to sleep for an hour or so, Uriah entered the old-fashioned parlor we used as a bedroom. "The telephone is for you. It's Stuart Caine. Jane's in labor."

I grabbed a flannel shirt from the chair. Uriah slid his hand down my back and then from waist to thigh as I passed him in the wide arched doorway connecting the living room to the parlor. "Nice outfit," he said.

"Hey, Stuart. Jane's in labor? How's she doing? How frequent are the contractions?" My mind and heart were racing.

"The contractions are about four to five minutes apart. They're getting harder."

Uriah had followed me into the kitchen. Standing behind me, he slipped his hands around my waist and pulled me close. I tried to push away his wandering hands and keep talking to Stuart without laughing. "Okay, Stuart. I should be able to get to your place by eight o'clock. See you then. Bye."

When I hung up the phone, Uriah suggested we go back to bed.

"Sorry." I turned in his arms and nuzzled into his warm neck. "Maybe later."

☙

On the ten-mile drive to Stuart and Jane's, I reviewed the steps of a delivery. I knew them cold. When I saw Promise in the distance, doubts began to creep into my mind. Why was I doing this? Why did I let Uriah talk me into joining this group? These people were willing to give up their livelihood and their old ways of viewing the world to move far from their homes and build an alternative community. I wasn't sure I wanted to give up so much, especially the ideals Uriah and I had developed together. Uriah didn't think Beatrice was right to say we should burn our "old tapes." We'd already burned our tapes once—the tapes of our religious childhood. What we had learned in the last five years was important to what we had become. *Those* old tapes we needed to keep.

I crossed my fingers when Zea was baptized. I couldn't honestly commit to what the church expected of me. I said the vows for the sake of the family. I might have to cross my fingers again if we were invited to become full members of Promise and take some sort of pledge. I didn't like the idea of taking a vow because there was no way to tell what I would believe in the future.

It was more than six months since we joined the group and we hadn't been officially accepted—maybe that was okay. Beatrice and Victor were having some kind of falling out and they weren't keeping up with applications and initiations.

Stuart was a believer. He had given everything to Promise and swallowed the philosophy in one big gulp as if it were the TRUE religion. I had misgivings about the dogma in *The Brotherhood's Promise*, just as I had misgivings about any religious dogma. I'd play with ideas, test them as if they were true. I nibbled, but in the end rarely took the bait. I loved the people at Promise—our new friends. I loved the social life, the school, practicing the virtues and reading and discussing all sorts of eclectic teachings. But . . .

As a kid I wanted to believe whole heartedly in the religion of my youth. My relatives and school friends seemed to have no doubts. I wished I could become so enthralled that I could walk to the front of a revival hall during the alter call and give myself to Jesus as my personal savior. My religious zeal was never ignited and it was a mystery to me how people could give up their sensibility to stories that couldn't possibly be true. Uriah was different. He was open to whatever new philosophy he read about.

Stuart not only was a true believer in Victor's fanciful stories, he was pious about it. Competitive in his devotion. Stuart's steadfast conviction was the reason I drove the ten miles to Promise to help him and Jane deliver their baby at home. Home birth was encouraged—actually it was expected. A subtle disapproval was levied against women who went to the hospital to have their babies. I hadn't been told specifically how this expectation developed, but there was much talk of how the medical establishment was incompetent, ruled by the drug and insurance companies, and should be mistrusted and avoided. It may have been Beatrice's personal soapbox, but without Victor around, she ruled. The overarching theme was this: the group must be self-reliant in order to survive the coming cataclysm.

Rumor had it, no, it wasn't rumor because Beatrice had told the story herself. She had delivered her daughter at home by herself eight years before. Her pelvic floor had torn and bled. Beatrice passed out on the bathroom floor. An infection set in and it took weeks for her to recover. Amazingly the baby thrived. In spite of the fumbled, avoidable complications of her delivery, Beatrice continued to preach the benefits of home birth and had assisted the women in the community during their deliveries.

Two months after Uriah and I arrived at Promise, at a potluck supper, a woman named Helen told the story of how she and her baby had almost died because Beatrice insisted she stay home even though the delivery wasn't going well. "Your karma and negativity are interfering," Beatrice had said. Helen and Peter eventually overruled her and went to the hospital. Helen had had a placenta previa—the placenta covered part of the birth canal. Helen was furious. Although Beatrice had stopped attending births at Promise, the women were still determined to have their babies at home with or without trained help. The potluck was Helen and Peter's goodbye party; they were leaving because of the authoritarian attitude of Beatrice and her core group.

While I understood the appeal of homebirth, I wouldn't consider it for myself without someone attending who knew what to do if something went wrong. Even with the gnawing worry that I was practicing outside the scope of my nursing license, I volunteered to be the community's midwife. Better that than refusing to help and hear later of needless trauma or even death. It was a dilemma in which I was not happy to be entangled. So, I studied incessantly, and had gained some confidence assisting with the successful deliveries of two Promise babies.

I pulled up to the house. Stuart was sitting on the porch step. He quickly rose and opened the car door as I gathered my supplies. "Thank you for coming," he said. "I'm glad you're here." This was a more cordial response than I expected. Other than asking me to attend the birth, Stuart had never spoken to me before. The coaching I insisted on before I agreed to be the midwife had only been with Jane. Stuart, apparently, had more important things to do. I shouldn't have let him get away with it.

Jane was leaning over the kitchen counter when I entered the house. "Oh, my God. I'm glad you're here."

"What's happening?"

"My water broke fifteen minutes ago and the contractions are awful."

"Come, lie down for a minute before you walk around too much. I want to check to make sure the umbilical cord didn't drop when your water broke. And, I want to check the baby's heart rate and your dilation too. As I checked Jane's cervix, I was jolted by a feeling of dread. Something wasn't right. This delivery was going to be rough.

Jane caught the flash of fear in my face. "What's wrong?" She sat up and grabbed my wrist.

Quickly trying to qualify the anxiety that I obviously had already passed on to Jane, I said, "It's too early to tell, but the head isn't engaged. I can bounce it up with my fingers. Your cervix isn't flattening out and it's still firm. I'd say your dilation is only two, maybe three centimeters. The contractions should be doing more since your water broke." I listened to the baby's heart rate. No problem there; a robust 128 beats per minute—a boy. Perhaps it was one of my premonitions, but more likely intuition based on my growing experience as a midwife. The lower the rate and the deeper the tone, the more likely the baby was a boy. I could just tell. "The baby is large and in the correct position." I talked to Jane with a hand on her taut belly waiting for a contraction.

"Another contraction is coming, Alodie,"

"Okay. Take a deep breath. Now three short breaths and one long one." I began breathing with Jane as I had taught her earlier. "The contraction sure feels strong enough to do the job."

Jane's friends, other people from Promise, brought lunch. We ate in the living room while Jane rocked in a chair. She suddenly groaned, "They're getting worse."

It had been four hours since I arrived and I still couldn't determine with certainty that any progress had been made. After checking Jane again, I called Stuart into the room and sat on the edge of the bed. "Jane. Stuart." I said carefully to each of them. "I think the baby's head is too big to fit through the pelvis. It just isn't descending like it should with the length and intensity of the contractions. I think you need to go to the hospital to be evaluated for a pelvic disproportion."

Stuart stood up, "No," he held his pointed finger inches from my face. "We're going to have this baby at home!"

I felt a rage building, a rage that frightened me. "You're willing, Stuart, to endanger your wife and your child because of some irrational adherence to some asinine idea that homebirth is sacred?"

"We just need to wait a little longer. This is a natural process. Women have always had babies at home," Stuart argued.

"And some women and their babies have died." I had rehearsed this very scene in my mind. "I can't be responsible for Jane or the baby being injured or worse." I started packing up my tools.

"Alodie, wait another half hour," Jane begged. "Please. It will happen. I know it will."

"Fifteen minutes," I compromised, knowing better. "Fifteen minutes, and then I'm leaving." But after ten minutes, I was alarmed when the baby's heart rate jumped. The baby was in distress. "Please, go to the hospital, Jane, please." I gathered my supplies and put on my jacket. It was time to leave.

Stuart came running through the door as I backed out of the driveway. "Okay!" he said, "Okay."

I helped Jane and Stuart get ready for the twenty-mile drive to the hospital. "I'll call the emergency room and try to talk to a doctor. The nurses will know what's happening by the time you get there." I chose not to go along. The nursing staff would take over and there was nothing more I could do.

I drove home while the afternoon faded into evening. I noticed spring had teased a hint of green into the grass, a hint of red into the tops of the silver maples, and when I glanced into the rearview mirror, I noticed the sun had teased a few more freckles onto my nose. I had done my best, even though Stuart and Jane were disappointed. I couldn't work miracles. I had been given the opportunity to practice many of the Great Virtues. Practicing the twelve Great Virtues was one of the better tenets of the group. We were taught to pick a virtue each week and to try to use it in everyday life. The Virtues were compassion, generosity, courage, patience, discernment, commitment, efficiency, precision, integrity, acceptance, humility and self-restraint.

I took a deep breath. Adrenaline had made me jittery. What an experience! Although not one to pray, I hoped Jane and the baby would be all right. My dilemma burned inside my heart. Should I be doing this?

Uriah had supper waiting when I arrived home. I read a chapter from *The Little House in the Big Woods* to Zea. Milo held tightly to his hammer and his blanket and fell asleep in my arms. I tucked the kids into bed and took a shower. I hoped to take Uriah up on the offer he had made that morning, but when I climbed into bed, the slightest catch in his breathing told me he was asleep.

Beats Going to Nam

The windshield wipers weren't able to keep up with the downpour, but Uriah drove on despite the lack of visibility. The crossroads were exactly a mile apart and made it possible to navigate even in this deluge. We pulled into the Cottonwood townhall parking lot at 6:25 p.m., only five minutes before the start of the Promise monthly dinner and dance. I was frantic because we were late, even though the rain was a legitimate reason. Adding to my dismay, I noticed when I lifted my skirt to avoid dragging it though a puddle, Milo had crumpled and smudged it with grubby hands before his drop-off at the Promise childcare house.

Uriah and I weren't the only late-comers. Andy ran toward us in a yellow tuxedo with ruffles showing at the neck and cuffs, and I whispered to Uriah, "He looks like a wet canary."

"Lovely evening for a ball," Andy joked. He had mastered another of the group's tenets, to be positive no matter the circumstances. Victor had introduced the idea that there were disincarnate souls—ghosts of the less evolved called, The Black Mentalists, who thrived on negativity. It was better to keep your chin up lest they pester you when alone in the dark. I thought staying positive was a good practice to ward off depression, but not because of ghosts.

When Uriah and I entered the hall, our friends waved us to their table. I was happy they had saved us a place. I thought because we were late, we might have to sit next to one of the core group fanatics who would quote *The Brotherhood's Promise* in response to any simple statement.

The linen tablecloths and Italian lights helped disguise the ordinariness of the Cottonwood town hall. Dingy photographs of dead mayors hung on the walls, the folding chairs were scratched and dented, and the hardwood floor was gray with age. As Uriah and I squeezed in at a crowded round table, I studied our new friends and wondered again, as I often did, what their reasons were for joining Promise. They were hippies in suits and tuxedos with shaved faces and short hair. They escorted their flower-children partners who wore ballgowns and beehive hairdos. What had happened to them?

Alex and Rita came from Michigan, they said vaguely that they needed a fresh start. Herman and Georgia liked the spiritual nature of the teachings—they came from Pennsylvania. There was another couple at the table, but introductions were delayed because the meeting had started. I knew in various ways, our friends had been lost, just like we were. We had in common a search for new connections after leaving home and old friends behind. Promise was beginning to feel like home. I was involved with midwifing, teaching the kids and attending discussion groups about the book, other occult ideas and science news. Promise was mentally and spiritually stimulating, and aside from the true believers who thought they ruled, the people were smart and funny and good.

I struggled with Victor and Beatrice's bourgeois rules—especially the stay-at-home mom rule. In the early years of our marriage, it had taken a lot of consideration and conversation for Uriah and me to overcome the sexist roles we had grown up with. We weren't about to give up the equality for which we had worked so hard, but I was willing to stay at home for a while because Milo was still a baby. I felt like I was bending the rules a little bit by working outside the home as the community midwife, but no one called me on it. Most of our new friends didn't cow-tow rigidly to Beatrice and Victor's teachings either—at least not in private. I couldn't bring myself to wear a formal gown and I didn't have thick enough hair for a beehive. I wore a velvet patchwork skirt and a silk blouse and put my hair up in a bun, like I usually did anyway. Uriah wore a suit jacket and tie—he looked formal enough.

The business meeting was brief. The delegated speaker touched on the school's enrollment and the progress being made on a new plastics factory. Dinner was served, and as a bowl of cooked carrots was passed around the table, Rita said, "Look at these carrots, who cut them on right angles? Whoever it was should know better—the life force is completely gone."

"What are you talking about?" Rita's husband, Alex, asked her.

"We learned this morning, didn't we, Alodie? Vegetables should be cut on an angle along their energy meridians because it causes less trauma to the poor things. They keep their life force longer and shouldn't be cooked to hell either."

"A knife does cut through vegetables more easily on an angle, but I don't know about the rest of it." I had been irritated that morning when several women, including myself, had volunteered to prepare the meal for dinner. A know-it-all whose name was something like Sunshine or Sunlight, was telling us the proper way to cut vegetables. "That woman, whoever she was, was so bossy."

"I don't know—there might be something to it." Georgia said, in a wispy almost inaudible voice. Her eyes were hidden behind her long, straight brown bangs.

"Well, there is something to everything," Alex said sarcastically.

"Rita threw a carrot at him from across the table, "Aren't you profound."

The dishes were cleared and the first record was eased onto the turn-table. "What kind of music is this?" Herman asked, "Sounds like a recording of the Lawrence Welk Show."

"Without the bubbles," I said. "And it's kind of a dumpy place for a ball."

"Your standards are too high, Alodie," Alex winked at me. "What did you expect from the Cottonwood town hall?"

"I wonder where Victor is?" Rita asked, as her eyes followed Andy in his yellow tux twirl Beatrice around in a waltz. She looked elegant in a green low-cut gown and emerald earrings; an extra poof adorned her usual French twist.

"We haven't seen Victor since the day of our first interview," Uriah said.

"Seems like Beatrice is in charge," Alex leaned back in his chair.

"Maybe that's why no one is getting permanent membership," Herman said. "We've been here eight months and haven't heard a word about being accepted as full members."

"Nor have we," Rita shook her head. "What's going on?"

"Victor and his book are the reason we came to Promise," bemoaned Uriah. "He's our connection to the Brotherhood. No one else claims to be able to talk to any of the adepts."

"That's because none of us have mastered the Great Virtues— we're such morons." Rita was angry, but no one commented for fear of being negative.

"Who wants to dance?" Alex said brightly.

I loved to dance, but like most of our friends, rock and roll was all I knew. Ballroom dancing was beyond me, but even so I couldn't listen to the music without the urge to dance. "Uriah, come on, we can try to waltz—all we need to do is stand there and rock back and forth."

"Yeah, right, as you drag me around. You know you can't follow, Alodie."

"I won't drag you around, Uriah, come on."

"I'll dance with you, Alodie." Alex stood up and walked around the table. "Okay with you, Uriah?"

"Sure, please."

"Since when can you waltz, Alex?" Rita asked.

"Another one of my secrets," Alex winked at Rita as he took my hand.

On the dance floor, Alex slipped his arm around the velvet waistband of my skirt and pulled me close. I was startled but didn't pull away as a quiver went through me. I quickly learned to follow Alex in swooping circles around the room. "You are amazing," Alex whispered into my ear when the dance ended. The statement seemed to infer something besides my ability to dance.

Stuart and Jane entered the hall as Alex and I walked back to our seats. Jane squeezed through the crowd toward me and held out the baby, "Meet Lincoln," Jane said. The baby looked healthy except for two remaining egg-shaped lumps on his head and a fading bruise on his right upper cheek—I looked at Jane questioningly.

"We're fine now, really." Jane had told me about her delivery over the phone, with the exception of the baby's injuries. After an unsuccessful attempt to use high forceps, that had left Jane with thirty stitches and a bruised baby, a cesarean was done. Lincoln was over nine pounds.

Stuart gave me an unexpected, clumsy hug, and handed me a gift. "Thank you, Alodie, thanks, so much."

When I returned to the table, it took a moment to get the gist of an animated conversation. We had met so many people in the last few months that I couldn't keep their names straight. A few single men had joined our group and I hadn't met the guy who was speaking. "I was down to 110 pounds, just below the weight limit," he said.

"How did you do it?" Rita asked.

"I fasted every other day or so, ate only vegetables and drank tea. It screwed up my sleep cycle for a while and I passed out a couple times. I even hallucinated once and it took weeks to recover, but I'm fine now—beats having to go to Vietnam."

"At least you didn't end up in a mental hospital for a year like Alex did," Rita said. "Tell them, Alex."

"No, you tell them."

"He pretended to be schizophrenic. He had practiced for six months and got so good at being delusional that when he went in for his army physical, they sent him to the emergency room. Then he pretended to be catatonic and was drugged and sent to the psych ward. He didn't get out until the war was over."

"Beats having to go to Nam."

"Oh, my God," Georgia said quietly and looked around at the group. "That's as bad as what happened to Hermie. He got out of the draft, but not on purpose. Tell them, Honey."

Herman, a little jumpy, with eyes that darted and were and always open wider than what seemed natural, began—- "I don't remember much of how it happened. I was at a party for a friend who was leaving for the war. Someone had put LSD into the punch which was already loaded with vodka. I poured the last of the punch from the bowl into my cup and don't remember anything that happened during the next twelve months."

"I think maybe the LSD sank to the bottom," Georgia added.

"I still have flashbacks."

"We had two kids—it was a horrible year." Georgia squeezed Herman's hand, "I'm glad he made it back to us."

The group was silent for a few moments—lost in our own memories of the Vietnam era. There were no veterans at this table. I looked around for a vet Uriah had recently met at work who had lost several of the men in his unit. The soldiers were all smoking pot—a past-time for those biding their time on active duty and who had no intention of killing anyone. He had just been relieved of his watch when the Vietcong ambushed the trench killing everyone. Uriah told me the guy seemed glib about the whole experience and I wondered if he had PTSD. Why wouldn't he?

The war had been an overarching influence in our lives—an ongoing worry. It was an influence that had diminished our trust in the government, in justice, and in humanity. I felt an aching sorrow listening to these stories. I had tried during those years to be happy in a messed-up world. Why did our friends have to participate in a war based on a threat drummed up by politicians, capitalists and by generals of the armed services? Were they just itching for a fight? Over what? Communism? The draft was real, but the cause for all of the heartache was questionable.

"How did you escape the draft, Uriah?" Rita asked. You didn't go, did you?"

"I tried to get conscientious objector status. I was raised in a Dutch Reformed community which was far from having a pacifist tradition, but I've always believed in pacifism—my Dad even vouched for me. I got a high number when Nixon and his team decided to put the lottery into effect, so I dropped my C.O. application and my college deferment. I was classified 1A for two months and by the end of the year when the draft board didn't get to my lottery number, I was a free man."

"I would have taken my chances too," Alex said, "but it wasn't an option for me. Before the lottery they were taking everyone without a valid deferment."

"Those three months when Uriah was 1A status were tense," I said. "His lottery number was 219 and the draft number didn't even get close. The troops were being cut back by then."

"Remind me what 1A status was? You could have been called up at a minute's notice, right?" Rita wondered.

"What year was that?" Georgia asked.

"Um, 1971? Uriah?"

"Yeah, that's right."

"Zea was just a baby. I worried about being alone on the north side of Chicago while I finished school," I said.

"I'm glad that mess is over," Rita sighed, "Funny, though. I wish there was a decent cause to get behind now. The world is fucking boring—unless you get your kicks out of streaking or disco dancing. I guess that's why we came to Promise—to do something unusual."

"I'll tell you what," Alex said, "I wouldn't mind streaking at the moment. I hate this tuxedo!"

I declined Alex's request for another dance because I didn't want my fantasies to get out of control like they tended to do. I could read into any flirtation as a come on. Was I making more out of his touchy feely dance moves than he meant? Alex was smooth with women, but there was probably no more to it.

It was one o'clock when Uriah and I walked into the farmhouse with sleeping children in our arms. Jane and Stuart's gift was a white stoneware pot painted with one blue flower—simple, but beautiful. I placed it admiringly on the top of the refrigerator and planned to use it for my favorite recipes.

"Are you happy, Hon?" I asked Uriah as we cuddled together listening to the rain against the bay window.

"Sure," Uriah answered without hesitation.

Uriah didn't catch the sadness in my voice as I continued, "I miss our old friends and having something bigger than ourselves to care about, like we did during the war. Promise seems like a playground in comparison. I think our new friends feel the same. Chances are, we'll never experience the same comradery or a time like that again."

"Are you kidding?" Uriah raised both arms as if commencing a sermon, "What could be bigger than starting a new civilization?"

Uriah's enthusiasm was unlimited.

A Ball of Fire

Finish the page you're working on Zea and then you can go outside. I'm gonna run downstairs to wring out the laundry. Keep your eye on Milo, okay?"

Zea went to school at Promise for three hours on Tuesdays and Thursdays. Today was Wednesday, Zea's day to study at home. She was five, kindergarten age, but she had shown so much interest in reading, I taught her early. I had bought a couple of books before we joined Promise to teach me how to teach her. Zea could read before her fourth birthday. With encouragement from Miss Carol, I was structuring Zea's education more formally. The theory on which the Promise school based their curriculum was that there were critical periods for learning certain skills—mothers were to watch for the signs of these skills and provide their kids with the right materials.

Milo was playing with his wooden nuts and bolts, a task that would occupy him for quite a while. He had great concentration if he was using his hands to manipulate small objects.

Our antique wringer washing machine agitated until manually stopped and the clothes had been in the rinse water for at least an hour. I began to feed them between the rollers. My thoughts drifted to Uriah who had been gone for three days. I was going stir crazy. Except for Miss Carol, I hadn't talked to anyone over five-years-old since Sunday. "Shit! Ouch!" While distracted by my thoughts, I had fed my dangling braid into the wringer with a couple of Milo's diapers. I slammed blindly at the release lever; my cheek was inches from being pinched.

It was ridiculous, but in that second I thought of Wile E. Coyote being flattened by a steam roller in a Bugs Bunny cartoon and laughed out loud. I really needed to tie up my hair when using the wringer—the same thought I had the last time this happened. Although dangerous for the inattentive, I liked the old washing machine. I liked learning old-fashioned ways and being self-sufficient, even if it was impractical and inefficient. We had an electric dryer to use in the winter when it was too cold to hang clothes outside. The dryer worked occasionally. Uriah thought it might have a loose wire. Someone would have to fix it before next fall. I lugged the basket of wet clothes up the steps, set it on the landing, and went to check on Zea's worksheet.

"I'm done, Mommy."

"Great, Sweetheart. All set to go outside?" I scooped up Milo, who protested being pulled from his toys without warning. I put him on one hip, the basket on the other, and went outside. He toddled after Zea to the garden. As I hung the wash on the line, I was mesmerized by a puddle in the driveway alive with yellow butterflies. My trance was broken when I saw Milo making a detour toward the puddle. "Oh no you don't, Buddy, not until I get your clothes off." While I was struggling with Milo and his bib overalls, I heard Zea shouting.

"Mommy, look!"

The old milk-house blocked my view and I couldn't see what she had discovered.

"Mommy, come quick. Zane Grey Cat is pooping out bunnies!"

"What?" Before I could get to the garden, I guessed what was happening. Pregnant Zane Grey was having her kittens, but why was she giving birth between the bush beans and the zucchini? "We need to find a box and some hay, Zea. See that pile of dead grass by the apple tree? I'll look for a box." Zea and I found three kittens covered with dirt. We wiped them off with a damp, clean diaper and put them and their mother in the shed.

In the meantime, Milo was mucking around in the puddle and his diaper, now saturated with muddy water, was sagging around his knees. "Forget this, Buddy." I unpinned his diaper and flung it toward the house. I finished hanging the wash and said to Zea, "I'm going to transplant my house plants after I tether the calf in some nice long grass."

"Mommy, can I watch the kittens?"

"Yes, but don't touch them. We'll wait until they're a little older."

I gathered my plants and six new clay pots and pulled them to the edge of the cornfield in the kid's wagon. The corn was about three inches tall—the rows stretched endlessly to the horizon. The dirt was perfect, black and soft. My root-bound plants would thrive in this dirt. I scanned the yard to check on the kids and saw a front moving in from the west—more rain.

Shortly after lunch, the wind shifted and cool gusts began whipping the clothes off the line. The storm was coming in fast. Layers of clouds were sliding under and over each other. I untied the calf and led her toward the shed. The rain began pelting the tin roof. "Come on, Mary! Come on." I stumbled into the house carrying two baskets of laundry, one on top of the other. The slam of the door was followed by an explosion of thunder. I tripped on the top step, tumbling the clothes onto the kitchen floor.

"Mommy!" Zea and I had no courage during wind storms—not since a tornado blew our house apart last summer. "Can we go in the basement?"

"Absolutely. Let's go." I kicked through the piles on the kitchen floor, grabbed Milo from under the dining room table, and rushed to the basement. I sat on the bottom step and watched the kids arrange empty baby food jars into lines and circles. I remembered every detail of the tornado and replayed it in my mind while nervously jumping at every burst of lightning and thunder.

Crack! I was shocked out of my reverie by a very close lightning strike. Zea came running. "That one was close." I held her shaking body as she dug her face into my shoulder. Another deafening rumble shook the house and a ball of fire flew downward past the basement window. Silence was followed by the smell of smoke.

"Is the house on fire, Mommy?"

"I don't think so, Sweetie. I think lightning hit the house and came down the lightening rod, but I need to check. Stay here, okay? Be brave. I'll be right back." I had to pry Zea's hands from my neck. I went outside in the downpour, ran around the house and looked at the roof, but didn't see smoke or flames. Another flash made me dive under the eaves. Zea was crying when I came in. "I know you're scared, but I need to go upstairs and check the bedrooms and the attic." I didn't smell smoke or see any fire and hoped the lightening rod had served its purpose. I returned to the basement and sat down on the wooden steps. I held Zea on one knee as the storm subsided. Milo, overdue for his nap, cried on the other knee.

"Hey you guys, I'm home."

"We're down here."

Uriah came to the top of the basement stairs, a big box in his arms. "What's going on, Alodie? Is everything okay?"

"Not really."

Bedraggled

The big box Uriah brought home was carpeted with plushy three-day-old leghorn chicks. He had picked them up from the farmer's co-op in Herscher after work. "I think we should keep them in the basement under a heat lamp for a week or so until I can get the chicken coop ready. We can watch them more closely."

"Can we play with them? Oh, little chicks, you're so cute." Zea was already reaching into the box.

"Be gentle, Zea," I said. She was very careful as she lifted a chick to her cheek. The little yellow feathered balls were moved into the calf's vacated room.

At breakfast the next morning, the toast popped up—the crust had burned. "Darn it!" I said.

Zea picked up on my frustration and eyeing the burned toast whined, "I'm not eating that."

"I'll scrape the edge a little and it will be fine," I didn't anticipate Zea's resolve.

"No, it won't! It's burned!" she shrieked.

"Oh, for crap sake, Zea. It's not that big a deal. We shouldn't waste food."

Uriah entered the kitchen. "What's going on?"

"The edge of the toast is burned and Zea is pitching a fit,"

I stood to retrieve the toast. "Ahh. My legs are killing me. They've been aching since Milo was born."

"Still?" Uriah asked.

"Every so often they hurt like hell. I feel so fat and out of shape."

"You look fine, Alodie, give yourself a little leeway, you had two kids."

"But it bothers me."

"I'm kind of tired of hearing about it."

"Screw you, Uriah. Sorry to bother you with my boring life."

"Alodie, come on."

"I'm really worried about my legs. I don't get why they hurt so much. Maybe I have varicose veins, but I can't see anything."

"You're kind of young for that, aren't you?"

"Pregnancy can cause it, no matter your age. Georgia said fasting for a couple of days clears out the toxins in your system and boosts the immune system. It helps to clear the gunk out of the blood vessels which might aggravate varicose veins. I don't see how the immune system and varicose veins are connected, but I think I might give it a try."

"I'll fast with you. It's supposed to be a good spiritual practice too."

I could see Uriah's brain light up.

"Gandhi did it, and Jesus."

"Some weekend, we should try it."

"I'm not eating it!" Zea said again, as I put the worked over toast on her plate.

Uriah warned, "Zea, eat the toast or you'll have to go without. The toast is fine."

"No. It's not!"

"Zea. Remember your chart," I said. "You'll get a check for arguing instead of a star for cooperating."

"I don't care!"

"To the Happy Chair. Right now." Uriah stood up, but Zea jumped from her chair more quickly.

"I'm not going to the Happy Chair. I'm going to the basement to play with the chicks."

"No, you're not."

Zea bolted through the kitchen door, just out of Uriah's reach, but he caught her at the head of the basement steps and picked her up screaming and kicking. He put her in the little red rocking chair in the far corner of the living room.

"She's been crabby lately," I said.

"Yeah. Seems like it."

"You know why?"

"Maybe she's picking up on my mood."

"What's wrong with you?"

"I don't know." I was unhappy, that's all—busy with the kids, but bored at the same time. "I don't have a life of my own, Uriah. I don't know who I am anymore."

Zea was crying in the living room. "You're mean. You hurt my feelings."

We ignored her. "Maybe Beatrice is right about spanking once in a while," Uriah said.

"I don't think so." I've always shied away from discipline, especially physical punishment. Uriah was firm and consistent about reinforcing good behavior and ignoring or separating the kids when they weren't being so good. Consistency was the key. I had a tendency to get sweeter and sweeter as Zea got more and more testy, but it rarely worked. If I was tired, consistency was impossible. I often argued with Uriah about his being so tough, but he was probably right. Even so, spanking seemed extreme. "Let's wait and see, Uriah. Okay?"

"You hurt my feelings, Daddy," Zea said again.

"You hurt mine, Zea," Uriah replied with little sympathy.

"Alodie. I need to run into Dwight this morning for chick feeders and waterers. I'm going to meet a guy at ten to pick up the rabbits. You need anything from town?"

"No, but you can return these library books—except this Yoga book. I'm not done copying the postures."

ଔ

"Zea. I'm going to run down the road a bit. Maybe my legs will feel better if I get more exercise. Will you play with Milo in the yard? I won't go far, just back and forth a little and I'll keep an eye on you."

I noticed the clover along the shoulder was thick and healthy, but within six feet of the cornfield the clover and weeds were dead – an overspray of herbicide. It probably got into the soil too and that's why my houseplants looked so sickly.

I was winded within minutes and didn't run nearly as far as I had planned.

Uriah came home with five rabbits. His plan was to donate his time, instead of tithing, by raising chickens and rabbits and then give the members of Promise a break on the price of eggs and meat. He felt like the jobs he was given at Promise were disorganized and menial, and he felt unappreciated. His work crew had built a new pole shed for a farmer who was quitting the chicken business. Uriah asked the farmer if Promise could have the old chicken barn if they would disassemble and move it.

"I've just had it," Uriah had ranted one day. "It wasn't easy to take down that old barn, or to build a new block wall and set the trusses. We were just about to put on the sheathing when that straight-line wind came up and blew the thing down. The crazy core group decided to abandon the project and have some halfwit bull-doze the foundation. What a waste! Beatrice's minions just don't give a shit. We're working ourselves to death and we never see our families. No one consulted me; we could have put the trusses back up. It was a bummer that it blew over, sure, but sixty trusses?"

Instead of the animals being cared for at Promise, Uriah had cleaned out our chicken coop and had built a big cage for the rabbits that could be moved around the yard. The rabbits would have fresh grass to eat in the summer. Uriah named the rabbits Joist, Rafter, Brace, Purlin and Stud.

CR

I enjoyed the community's social gatherings. This month the decoration committee had made a special effort to brighten the neglected town hall. The candles added a soft sparkle to the room. Promise members were relaxed and didn't worry as much about being virtuous. As we ate our cheesecake dessert, we were quieted momentarily by its smooth splendor. The hubbub in the room had smothered the sound of distant thunder and gentle rain on the roof.

The candles flickered when a small man with a dripping fedora pulled low over his forehead opened the double doors at the back of the hall. The wind flapped the tails of his tan trench-coat which was buttoned snuggly under his chin. I had my back to the doors, like half the people in the room, but quickly saw the ardent expressions on the faces of those across the table and turned around.

Victor removed his hat and moved with focused vision up the aisle to the front of the room. Recognition deadened the hall in waves of silence. Victor stepped to the core group's table and faced Beatrice directly. With a voice of force and resolve, he said, "I formally request that you rescind Resolution 221." Breathing in the room stopped while we waited for revelation, but none came.

Beatrice rose. With the menace of Medusa, she hissed, "Never, under any circumstances."

"Holy Shit!" Andy couldn't hold back.

"What is going on?"

"What is Resolution 221?"

"The board kicked Victor out of the group."

"They did what?"

"Why?"

The dance that followed dinner was subdued and broke up early. Victor had walked back down the aisle and into the rain after Beatrice stood her ground. "She was pissed. That's for sure," Rita said.

╏

At three o'clock in the morning, I woke up when Uriah returned to bed.

"What were you doing, Hon?"

"Didn't you hear the storm?"

"No, I was seriously tired when we got home."

"I went to check on the chicks and found water seeping into the basement. The ground must be saturated from all the rain we had this week. The chicks were perched on the two-by-four across the door of the room and one fell off and drowned. I hope you don't mind, but I put the rest in a box in the corner of the kitchen." He put a bedraggled chick on his pillow.

"Of course not, but what's with this chick?"

"This one doesn't look so good. I think I'll let it sleep here so it doesn't get smothered by the others."

"What if it gets smothered by you?"

"It will be fine. Night."

"Night, silly."

Always early to rise, Uriah lifted my pillow and pulled the covers from my shoulders.

"Uriah, what the heck?"

"I can't find the chick."

"What chick?"

"The one I brought to bed last night."

"Oh, yeah." I got out of bed and helped Uriah peel back the sheets and the white chenille bedspread. We found the chick more than bedraggled. It was dead under the bed.

The chicks stayed in the kitchen until the smell of their poop overpowered the smell of the pancakes.

Two-Hundred Twenty Volts

ventured into the basement deluge only once, the morning after the chicks had been evacuated. Uriah had left early for work. As the day dragged on, I became obsessed with the idea that the old wiring in the house could short out, or I might be alone for three days without power, or worse, that a fire might start. I also needed to get the bag of chicken feed out of the basement. I brought two kitchen chairs downstairs and created a portable bridge. I stood on one chair, moved the other into place a little further along, stepped on the second and moved the first until I reached my goal. My innovation worked, although moving a twenty-five-pound sack of grain by this method was painstakingly slow.

What did I think I was going to do about the wiring anyway? I didn't know what I was looking for or what to do if something looked dangerous. Amid the bobbing baby food jars that had drifted from the lines and circles of the kid's lightning storm project, I maneuvered the chair bridge into the cellar and looked at the fuse box. The wiring was in the ceiling and the water heater had been set up on cement blocks. This basement had a history of flooding—no doubt.

The electric outlet for the wringer washer and the 220-volt outlet for the dryer were attached to a piece of plywood hanging from a ceiling joist. "Looks okay to me," I said to myself and gradually made my way, one chair after the other, back to the basement steps.

The following week, I had to do the laundry. Milo was out of diapers and I was out of underwear. The smell from the diaper pail was pervasive. I would have gone to the laundromat in Dwight, but the week had been busy. Uriah and I had gone to his mom's on Friday night to drop off the kids so we could go to Andy's wedding on Saturday. We had met Rita and Alex at the interchange of I-57 and Highway 17 in Kankakee on one of the hottest days of the summer.

As I loaded the washing machine, I cringed. Had it been a good idea to disclose our experiment with open marriage to Alex and Rita? Then, my mind wandered to the discussion we had about Andy's fiancée's name.

"Do you think Sunshine is her real name?" Rita said, folded into the black vinyl seat of our hatchback Chevy Vega. She fanned herself with an Egg McMuffin carton. "Can you just hear it? Andy and Sunshine, I pronounce you man and wife. Would you guys roll down the windows up there?"

"I suppose, if it isn't her real name, we'll find out this afternoon," Uriah said.

"What other name would suit her as well?" Alex asked and answered. "Airhead? Dingbat?"

"Maybe her name was Cornelia and she just had to change it. Be nice," I said.

I gathered dirty clothes from around the house and carried damp, rank armfuls down the steps. I looked around the house—what a mess. My plants were now beyond saving. Toys were strewn everywhere. The dining room table was littered with mail, Zea's books, and art projects. The kitchen counters were piled high with dirty dishes. I pushed my red bandana up on my forehead. "I need to wash my hair," I had started to talk to myself for lack of adult interaction. I remembered my failed attempt to look nice for Andy's wedding.

The midwestern/midsummer heat had wilted my curled hair within twenty minutes after I took it out of the rollers. I had pulled up the sides and secured them with a barrette, but it kept slipping. I had yet to find a barrette, aside from a child's plastic neon butterfly, that was small enough to hold my fine silky hair.

The basement floor was still wet, but there was no standing water anywhere. I sorted the clothes and started the washing machine. Zea came to the top of the steps. "Mommy? Can we do a project?"

"I don't think so, Honey. I need to catch up around the house. Maybe we can make up a cleaning game. What do you think?" I leaned over to pick up a sock and reached to the dryer for balance. Two hundred twenty volts of electricity sent me flying and screaming through the air and into an eight-inch square post. I sank down into a pile of Uriah's dirty work jeans.

"Mommy? What are you doing? Why did you scream?"

I could say nothing for a few seconds until I gained my senses and equilibrium. "There's a short in the dryer."

"The dryer's short?"

"Never mind, Zea. I got an electric shock. I'm okay, I think." I went upstairs to check myself over for burns but found none.

"Alex, can you come over to help me? I got a bad shock from the dryer. The washing machine's running and I'm afraid to go downstairs." Alex was the only electrician I knew. He mentioned at the dance he had time off because he was between jobs. While waiting, I frantically tidied up the house and tried to make myself look less frazzled.

The trip to the wedding came into my head again. The memory made me shudder. My curiosity sometimes bordered on nosiness and it prompted me to find out more about Rita and Alex.

"So, Alex. You were in a rock band before you came to Promise, right?" I didn't wait for a response before adding, "You're from Michigan?"

"Yes, and yes." Alex paused.

"Thanks for the details," I had hoped to get more information than that. At least enough to start a conversation, but I sensed a sudden tension in Alex.

He continued, "Kind of a sore subject." The conversation halted momentarily.

"Alex gave up the band to marry me," Rita finally broke the silence.

Alex and Rita gave us just enough information to make it nearly impossible to drop the subject. Uriah couldn't resist. "Because?"

"I was a bit out of control back then."

"I would say more than a bit," Rita continued. "We were living together and our baby had already been born. Alex had a woman—and a supplier—in every town where he had a regular gig."

"But tell them, Rita, you were getting a little extra on the side once in a while too."

"But that was different. I had a relationship on and off during college with a professional football player. We were pretty serious, but our backgrounds were different. The little differences became big irritations. We tried to cut it off because we just couldn't live together, but we had an emotional connection and it wasn't that easy."

Another pause. It seemed like that was all the information we were going to get.

"And now it's your turn. Any secrets you're willing to tell?" Alex looked at Uriah across the front seat and I waited to see if he would spill anything. He didn't hesitate.

"Alodie and I have an agreement and I guess it's still in effect. Alodie?"

"I don't know. We haven't talked about it for a long time."

Uriah continued, "We were married young, especially Alodie; she was seventeen. After a couple of years, we both became curious what it would be like to have a relationship with someone else. We were pretty tight and on an intellectual level it seemed workable."

I pulled myself forward using the back of the bucket seat. "It seemed to me that loving a second person wouldn't take love away from the first person."

"Sounds pretty naïve, Alodie. What about the second person?" Rita leaned forward as well. "Wouldn't the new guy get sort of a bad deal? I mean, from the beginning you would have no intention of breaking up your marriage. What would be in it for him?"

"A little excitement, a little love, a little diversion," Uriah said. "Just like it was for us. The only trouble was that it started to wear on us. The one having the encounter had all the fun and became distant for a while, distracted. It got emotionally complicated."

"That must be an understatement. Didn't you get crazy with jealousy?" Rita asked.

"I got jealous," I admitted, "but it seemed like Uriah felt lonely more than jealous. Right Hon?" I didn't give Uriah time to answer. "I tried not to feel jealous because I knew there wasn't a chance we would break up, but I'm terrible at controlling my emotions."

"You felt that sure of your relationship?" Alex seemed amazed; his voice inflected. He even squeaked.

"Yep. Still do." Uriah reached back to pinch my leg, but pinched Rita's by mistake. "Oops. Sorry, Rita."

"Man, you two are something else," Alex looked into the rearview mirror and smiled at me.

Through the parlor window, I saw a car approach. Alex. My heart raced a little. Why was I so jittery about Alex coming over? "Get a grip, Alodie," I said to myself.

"Hey, Alex."

"Hey to you. Are you all right? The dryer is on a two-twenty. You could have been killed."

"I didn't need to know that. I suppose because I touched it with my left hand, the shock didn't go through my heart."

"Good planning." Alex put his arm around my shoulder. "Really, Alodie, I'm glad you're okay."

Alex pulled out the fuses and began working on the dryer. We talked about the wedding. I pictured the scene only half listening to Alex chatter while he worked.

South of the Champaign/Urbana exit we turned west. The corn was wilting in the noon heat just like my hair and the horizon was cloaked in a humid haze.

"I'm stuck to the seat," Rita complained, rearranging her spaghetti-strap dress and her long legs.

"We better sing through the songs a couples of times, we're almost there," Alex said.

"And when at first I met you, I didn't know your name." Alex, Uriah and I sang together.

"Ha," Uriah said, "the song fits, doesn't it?"

"Sure does," Rita agreed. "Sunshine? Get real."

As we descended the stone steps into a sunken garden fifteen minutes later, I asked, "How did Andy find out about this place? It's beautiful."

"He has connections," Rita said. "He goes all over the area setting up his beehives and selling honey. I heard Sunshine say the old estate was willed to the county to be preserved as a park. This garden used to be a private playing field. Look over there where the chairs are set up, it looks like an old tennis court."

Vines hung from the surrounding stone walls and a small water fall emptied into a pond bordered with cattails and lily pads. I walked to the moss-covered wall and buried my nose in an open rose. The guests were from Promise, except a few, and I guessed by the curly hair and flamboyance of the strangers, they were Andy's family.

Alex was talking about Andy from behind the dryer. "Why did Andy and Sunshine decide to get married all of a sudden? You suppose she's pregnant?"

"Maybe. Andy was just dating someone else last month. Do you think, if Sunshine is pregnant, that it's Andy's baby?"

"Andy's known for getting around. Actually, so is Sunshine. It's anybody's guess." I watched Alex as he worked. He was movie-star handsome with blond wavy hair and gentle features. I wondered what he looked like when he played in his band; he had much longer hair for sure. "But if Sunshine is pregnant, it must be Andy's, he wouldn't marry her otherwise, would he?"

The wedding ceremony had been simple—performed by a justice of the peace. I laughed as I remembered singing the last line of our song, "… the things you do endear you to me. Ah, you know I will …" Then, the justice of the peace said, "Andrew Jackson Brown and Agatha Gail Blakeley, I pronounce you man and wife." Rita had winked at me from her place in the second row.

"What's so funny?" Alex asked.

"Just thinking about Agatha Gail Blakeley."

"There." Alex plugged in the dryer and slapped the top, "Fixed."

"Thanks, Alex."

"Anytime. I love seeing you." His disc-jockey tone made me a little uneasy and I was relieved when he declined my offer for coffee. "Alodie, I'd love to stay, but I've got to put in some hours at Promise today."

As I opened the door for Alex, he leaned over and kissed me on the cheek. I stared down the road long after the car was out of sight.

Plucking Feathers

I t was a Saturday morning in late August and the leghorn cockerels were ready to butcher. The pullets and one young rooster named, Spurs, would be spared for eggs and breeding.

Uriah and I had never butchered chickens before, so Georgia and Hermie were coming over to help. Georgia thought learning the anatomy of chickens would be an excellent home-school lesson for her kids—Zeb, Louise and Opal.

I had put my two blue-speckled canning pots on the stove and set the water to boiling before our guests arrived. The dead chickens would be dunked into the water in order to loosen their feathers. The plucking would take place in the far end of the kitchen. The featherless birds would be thrown out the window into a garbage can filled with ice water. The birds would cool down and be gutted, washed and packaged. Uriah had moved the picnic table close to the house for this process. Another garbage can would be used for the unwanted remains.

"Here they come!" screamed Zea, flying into the kitchen. She had stood by the road next to the mailbox for at least fifteen minutes waiting anxiously for her friends. She had been anticipating "butchering day" since she heard the plan, pretending to be Laura from *The Little House in the Big Woods*. I gave Zea a hug, her excitement was catchy. She had deliberated over what to wear for the occasion and looked adorable in the red flower-print dress she had chosen.

"Come on in. I've got breakfast ready," I greeted our guests as they walked toward the door. "Then we can start the procedure. Zea, will you run to the shed and get Daddy?"

"So, this is the farmhouse," Hermie looked around. "You didn't understate its size. It's huge."

"Crazy, isn't it? I'll give you a tour later. We don't even use the three bedrooms upstairs and we're still swimming in space."

"I'll bet it's tough to heat." Hermie looked at the tall, double-hung dining room window.

"It is, and the wind finds every crack. I'm not looking forward to another winter in this place, although I love living in the country."

"We have the same problem in our house," Hermie said, as he roamed into the living room.

"This dining room set is beautiful." Georgia ran her hand along the smooth dark reddish-brown finish of the buffet.

"Uriah's grandfather just moved into a rest home; this furniture was his. I placed the silverware around the table. Uriah's uncle wants it someday, but doesn't have room in the house he has now. In the meantime, we get to use it."

"Is it antique? Anything special?"

"I think it's a Duncan Phyfe replica, if that means anything. I don't know much about furniture. It looks a bit out of place with our collection of junk. I hope we can keep it in good condition. I prefer furniture the kids can jump around on; we'll have to be careful with this stuff."

"I agree," Georgia said. "Furniture should be usable. I'd hate to nag the kids all the time to keep their feet down. We have a couch, though, that's been jumped on way too much. When we sit on it our butts almost hit the floor."

I made whole wheat apple fritters for breakfast—Zea's favorite. The conversation focused on Promise, as it often did when our friends were together. "Did you guys hear Beatrice is leaving the group and taking a bunch of her followers with her?" Hermie asked.

Georgia rolled her eyes, "Hermie always hears the latest gossip before anyone else does, and he loves to pass it on."

"Gossip can't be on the list of Virtues, Hermie," I teased.

"No, but it sure is fun."

"Do you think Beatrice leaving Promise has anything to do with Resolution 221?" Uriah wondered. "I'm in the dark about what that's all about."

"God, wasn't that a freaky meeting? I still haven't gotten over it. Victor and Beatrice don't seem to like each other much."

"It has everything to do with Resolution 221," Hermie said. "The board kicked Victor out and he wants back in."

"What happened?"

"Victor did something major to piss Beatrice off, but no one in the know is telling."

"Do you think they'll let him back in?" Uriah asked.

"I heard at the school," Georgia said, "that someone overheard Beatrice say, 'It's him, or me'."

"Who told you that?" Hermie asked.

"Rita."

"Why didn't you tell me, Georgia?"

"Because you would spread it everywhere."

"Where has Victor been all this time?"

"In Texas."

"In Texas? What's he doing there?"

"Beats me."

Uriah said, "We better get started. It's going to be a long day."

I pushed my chair from the table and my long skirt caught under the leg. The pitcher of orange juice I had picked up splashed onto the brocade upholstery of the chair. "This crazy dress code, skirts and fancy furniture are totally impractical."

"Forbearance, Alodie," Uriah teased.

"Right."

"Shall we?" Hermie got up from the table.

"Can I watch, Daddy?" Zea grabbed Uriah's hand.

"I don't think so, Zea, you better stay here and help Mom and Georgia. Why don't you show the kids around? Maybe they want to play with the rabbits; I put the cage under the apple tree."

"But Daddy, I want to see the chickens run around with their heads chopped off."

"Zea, we're not doing it that way. We're going to hang them by their feet so they can't run around. It's important to respect the animals we use for food, and thank them."

"How are you doing with the astral travel lesson?" Georgia asked me while we washed the breakfast dishes.

"I've been practicing every night. I tell myself to wake up five minutes before the alarm and usually do wake up just before it rings, but I haven't flown to other realms. How about you?"

"Same for me, but I did have an astral experience once. It was after Louise was born—I was exhausted. I had hemorrhaged and was anemic. I was on the couch just falling asleep when I seemed to look down on myself. It felt like I was floating with my back touching the ceiling—frightening, but fascinating. The next thing I saw, still floating along the ceiling, was Louise in the bedroom. She was whimpering. I woke up back in my body and went to check on her—she *was* whimpering. That happened three years ago before we came to Promise. It was one of the reasons why the book intrigued me so much. I haven't had any luck repeating the experience, but I do wake up, like you, just before the alarm."

"Maybe it's a matter of practice." I lifted the lid from one of the pots on the stove; it was boiling and I turned down the flame. "I wonder if physical stress or sickness makes astral travel more likely?"

"Maybe. This is your first-time plucking chickens?" Georgia asked, as she pulled the wet dish towel through the refrigerator handle.

"Yep," I replied.

"You're going to love the smell."

"Yucky!" Louise squealed, as the first chicken was lifted, dripping from the pot.

"P.U.!" said her older brother, Zeb.

Milo stood between my legs and fiddled with the chicken's feet as I twisted handfuls of dirty feathers from the bird, "What do you think, Honey?"

Milo never said much, but his grunt and smile showed me he thought this was a pretty cool project. In a minute, he was pulling feathers too. "Careful, Milo, not too hard, if you pull too hard the skin will tear."

"You're so patient, Alodie," Georgia said as she watched me show Milo how to pull gently.

"I'm okay when the kids show an interest in things, but I don't have any patience for whining."

"Who does?"

"We better start gutting these birds," Uriah said when he came in for a drink of water. "The garbage can is full, so why don't you finish this bunch and then we can work together for a while outside. I'll get the knives."

"We'll have to do the final wash inside, won't we Uriah?"

"Yeah, I guess so. This is quite an ordeal, huh?" Uriah kissed me on the cheek as he passed the table, "You smell like a chicken, Alodie."

"Thanks, Pal."

"Gross!" Louise said, as Hermie slit a bird's lower belly and pulled out the intestines. After scraping the lungs out through the opening at the throat, he wiped the slime from the bird's windpipe. "Listen to this," he said, holding it to his lips. He blew through the trachea and it sounded like a pathetic cockle-doodle-doo.

"Cool," Zeb said. "Can I try it?"

"Don't you want to wash it off?" Georgia asked.

"It's okay," Hermie said, "these birds were healthy."

"Can I try it?" Zea asked. "I'm gonna wash mine."

Soon all the kids, Opal and Milo included, were prancing around the yard pretending to be roosters. "Is this disrespectful?" Uriah wondered.

"I think it's okay, they sure are having fun," I said. "Pass me one of those, will you?"

"Have you guys heard a new couple came to Promise last week who are opening a piano salvage shop?" Hermie asked, as he pulled the last chicken from the ice water. "I'd love to work there."

"You play some jazz piano, don't you?" Uriah asked.

"I play some. I'd like to learn how to fix pianos. I think the shop is going to be set up in Kempton which is only eight miles from our place. How is your job going, Uriah?"

"Not great, actually. The pay is low and I'm gone a lot. I've been thinking about starting my own carpentry business. I may put in a bid on a job in Lockport—an Italian barber wants to renovate an old building for a salon."

"Well, if you do start a business and need help, let me know. I'm tired of working at Promise and being bossed around by know it all, know nothings."

Uriah agreed, "I try to avoid working there if I can help it. Did you hear they bull-dozed the barn we were building?"

"Yeah, what a waste." Hermie threw the last of the chicken guts into the tub, "Looks like we're done."

"Anyone want a beer?" I asked.

"Absolutely!" Georgia said. "I'm glad Promise doesn't prohibit alcohol, but I sure do miss my smokes."

By six o'clock, Uriah and Hermie had singed the last bit of fuzz from the skins of the chickens, wrapped them and put them in the freezer. "We better get home," Georgia said. "The kids are winding down. Are you going to Andy and Sunshine's party tomorrow?"

"We're planning on it," Uriah said. "We haven't jammed much since we came to Promise."

"I hope Andy has a piano." Hermie stuck his head out of the open kitchen window and yelled, "Come on, kids, we're ready to go."

Too Many Sad Times

The potluck and party had been planned for making music. Andy played the string base, Alex the guitar, Hermie the piano and Uriah switched between the banjo and bass. There were other musicians who floated in and out of the jam. The ratio of men to women at the party was at least two to one, which about matched the ratio at Promise.

I was in the kitchen to help Sunshine set out the food. She was swirling lemon pudding in a blender and Zea was drawing at the table. As Sunshine stepped to the refrigerator to get another egg, a shimmying blender came into Zea's peripheral vision and she let out a hawk-like shriek, "It's gonna fall off!" Filled almost to the brim, the blender was precariously balanced on the edge of the counter.

"Zea," Sunshine said, with a reproving wave of her hand from behind the refrigerator door, "The blender won't fall off if you don't think it will." Zea looked at me—confusion with a touch of anger crinkled her face. My lunge was a second too late.

"Oh, my God!" I was splattered, as was most of the kitchen with sticky yellow pudding. I couldn't help but laugh. What else was there to do? The energy meridians of carrots? Thoughts able to stop runaway blenders? Seriously, Sunshine.

I took Zea, as she licked her forearm, to the bathroom. As she ruined her appetite, I dabbed the pudding from our clothes and we went back into the kitchen. I noticed through a window that Zea's friends had arrived. "Off you go, Honey, Louise and Zeb are on the tire swing."

Sunshine was at the table, her head down crying, so I closed the kitchen door. "Hey, I'll help you and we'll have this cleaned up in no time."

Sunshine continued to sob. I put my arm around her shoulder, "Hey, you okay? It's just pudding."

"You're right, it's just pudding, but I'm kind of strung out." Sunshine stood up and grabbed my arms, I could feel her sinking.

"What is it? What's wrong?"

"I need to tell someone. Can you keep it to yourself?"

"Of course."

"Andy asked me to have an abortion right after we got married and I finally did it three weeks ago. I'm really sorry now. We barely talk to each other."

"Wow," was all I could say.

"It was really sweet of Andy to marry me, especially because I didn't know for sure whose baby it was, but I didn't expect him to ask me to get an abortion. Why would he want to marry me if that was his intention all along?"

"I doubt if it was his intention all along; he truly wanted to marry you, but maybe he had second thoughts afterwards. Did you tell him you weren't sure he was the father?"

"I think so, but he claims I didn't make it clear."

"But it wasn't clear," I said, but now the picture was coming into focus.

"You think Andy misinterpreted what you said?"

"Maybe, yeah, I might have been purposely vague. It was stupid of me to marry Andy. Everything went so fast and he had just broken up with Irene. I was probably a rebound security blanket for him—he was for me, that's for sure."

Rita poked her head through the kitchen door. She noticed Sunshine's tears and the pudding splashed everywhere. "Sorry," she said and ducked back out.

"It's okay," Sunshine said. "Come on in, Rita. I overreacted to this mess."

"Let's call the dogs in here," Rita said. "We'll get this mess cleaned up in no time." Supper was ready within minutes after Andy's two golden retrievers left the kitchen.

The women sat on the porch and we watched the sun go down. In the living room, the musicians sang, "No use crying, talking to a stranger, tellin' the sorrows you've seen. 'Cuz there are too many bad times and too many sad times and nobody knows what you mean." The four-square farmhouse was built on a rise—considered a hill by the locals. A lone cottonwood tree to the west of the house stood in silhouette against the amber of the setting sun. Zea and the other kids from Promise were rolling down the hill as was a boy I didn't recognize, dressed in a cat suit.

We heard a commotion in the house and in unison twisted our bodies and eyes toward the sound. "Now what?" Rita said. Then I heard Milo begin to wail. He liked hanging around his dad, so I had left him in the house. I flew into the living room before Uriah had a chance to react. Blood sputtered from Milo's mouth along with his sobs. I scooped him into my arms and tried to assess the damage. His teeth were intact. Uriah had to hold Milo's flailing arms for me to check his tongue, which looked okay.

Uriah said, "I think Milo saw that wrench over there on the book shelf. He took off on a run and ran right into the coffee table."

Fifteen minutes and two bloodied washcloths later, I found the piece of skin that held down Milo's top lip had been severed. "Is this little piece of skin necessary?" I asked. Speculation was limited to a synchronized group shrug—the musicians were busy again.

A tall, wisp of a woman, with curly red hair and a freckled face watched as I settled into the porch swing with Milo. "What happened to him?" the woman asked. I was surprised by her nasal low-pitched voice. The woman squatted to Milo's level and he immediately hid his face against my chest.

"He cut the skin that holds down his upper lip. It bled so much that I couldn't see what happened right away."

"Guy did that a couple years ago."

"Did it cause any problems?" I asked.

"Oh, no, it healed just fine." The woman reached out to touch the top of Milo's head, "You'll be okay, Buddy. What's your name?" Milo recoiled even further from the invasion of the touch.

"His name is Milo." I answered for him—it wouldn't be in character for him to answer himself.

"Hi Milo, I'm Cass Scarlatti. That's my son, Guy, in the cat suit. My husband, Seamus, is over there by the tire swing."

"The guy petting the dogs?"

"Yeah."

Rita had been listening, "Well, isn't he gorgeous!"

"Geez, Rita! I'm Alodie. This is Rita."

Rita extended her hand, "Welcome to Promise, Cass. Sorry, I was overwhelmed. He is handsome!"

"I know he is."

"When did you arrive?"

"Last week."

"Has Seamus found work?"

"Yes, he was hired to manage the plastics factory."

"Moved right into the upper ranks," Rita raised her eyebrows. "That's great."

My attention drifted back to Sunshine. Where was she? Milo wiggled to get free and I let him run toward the other kids, "Watch where you're going, Sweetheart." I excused myself from the conversation and went into the house to look for Sunshine. Alex came out of the upstairs bathroom and we met in the hall.

"Alodie, hey."

"Hey to you, Alex."

"I wish I could see more of you without these crowds around all the time." Alex put his hands on my shoulders just as Sunshine opened a bedroom door and set a suitcase in the hall. Alex pulled away quickly and went down the steps and I followed Sunshine back into the bedroom.

"What are you doing, Sunshine?"

"I need to get away."

"Do you have a place to stay?"

"I'll go to my sister's in Chicago until I can think more clearly."

"I hope you're okay. Keep in touch, will you? We have to go before the kids get tired."

"Yeah, I'll try."

I left the bedroom and gathered our belongings which were strewn around the kitchen, the living room and the yard. Uriah had already packed his instruments. On the way home, I told Uriah about Sunshine and Andy. "Do you think Sunshine will ever come back?" Uriah wondered.

"I doubt it," I closed my eyes and let my head drop back onto the car seat. "Uriah?" I paused.

"Yeah?"

"Alex came on to me again. He caught me at the top of the steps."

"And?"

"Nothing ... I don't know. He's attractive."

"You gonna do anything about it?"

"I'm not planning to."

Spirits

leaned over the steering wheel and tried to spot the moon through the windshield. I could see the big dipper, and Orion was rising in the east above the fields plowed open for winter.

The sweet, earthy smell of cows, milk, manure and sileage seeped through the vents of the car as I passed the only dairy farm that still existed in the area. The scent was rare, a remnant of a life that used to be common on the Illinois prairie, now almost extinguished, lost in a vast sea of odorless corn and soybeans.

A stone wishing well at the intersection marked the turn onto Highway 17, 25 miles west of Kankakee. Without snow or wind, I could relax and let my thoughts wander into the imaginary romance with Alex that occupied my times of idle mind. This fantasy wasn't a good past-time. Fantasies could come true if enough thought and visualization was tossed into the universe; this tenet of the group I believed. I had jeopardized my relationship with Uriah once before with an imagined romance that had become a reality.

Thirty minutes later, I was plunged into the present when I saw the pointed wings of a maiden moon pierce the horizon. A bank sign flashed 10:40 p.m.; there was time to spare as I turned north along the Kankakee River and pulled into the hospital parking lot. Anxiety needled through my veins as it always did when I arrived at work.

I defied the restraint Promise asked of women who had children, and took a job at the Kankakee hospital on the graveyard shift every other weekend. A break from domesticity had become necessary for my sanity, and we needed the extra money.

While the evening nurses finished their paperwork, I started rounds with a nursing assistant. We would have a one-break night at best.

I felt the smooth coolness of my silky uniform and heard the soft rustle it made as I walked down the long hallway. World War II vintage, it was old but never worn, a treasure I found at a Salvation Army thrift store. The mid-calf length skirt and the three-quarters sleeves were classy and fit my tall frame perfectly. My white nylons, grandmother style lace-up nursing shoes, and my winged hat with the black stripe added to what I thought a real nurse should look like—authentic—like Florence Nightingale.

Jen, my nursing assistant, was more practical and wore white tennis shoes, white pants and a white blouse that accentuated her curly black hair. She had come from the Virgin Islands the year before and was attending Olivet Nazarene College to be a nurse or a teacher, she hadn't decided for sure.

Mr. Allen's call light was flashing and we entered his room. "I'm so uncomfortable, could you girls roll me to my side?" he asked.

"Of course, would you like a drink of water?" Jen offered.

"No, just roll me over. I'm so tired, but I can't seem to fall asleep while I'm on my back."

"Would you like anything more for pain, or something to help you sleep?" I knew bone cancer was extremely painful and I wasn't concerned whether Mr. Allen was due for his pain medication because if he needed it, it was the right time.

"No, I don't think so, I'd just like to try a different position."

"Your family will be comin' in de mornin'," Jen's words slipped into the rhythm of the Caribbean.

"I'd like to die before they come so they don't remember me like this."

"Oh, Mr. Allen, they'll want to be here with you." The words caught in my throat as I remembered how Uriah and I felt six months earlier when Uriah's father died suddenly before we could say goodbye.

"Okay, are you ready? We'll turn you on the count of three. One, two, three." While keeping his spine straight, Jen and I turned Mr. Allen to his side. He groaned quietly, took a rattled breath, and stopped breathing. We waited a moment, looked into each other's eyes and eased him to his back. Gradually, Mr. Allen's face relaxed and a hint of a smile enlightened his face, he was no longer in pain. Jen and I stood at the side of the bed for a moment with tears in our eyes and I said in a whisper, "He seems happy— he just drifted away."

Jen looked intently at the window, walked to the door and glanced down the hallway. "Yes," she said, "he is happy." Her behavior seemed a little odd, but not enough for me to think about it twice.

It was three o'clock and the light in the break room was dim. The colors were barely discernible. The coffee, made for a midnight break, was burned, but we didn't have time to make a fresh pot. Jen and I sat down in a booth and realized simultaneously we had been walking the hospital floors for four hours. We sighed with relief as our legs went up on the opposite seats and we sat quietly for a moment. Jen said, "Mr. Allen was so relieved to die."

I agreed, "I can't get over the smile on his face—it's been haunting me all night."

"Yeah, and then the way he wandered over to the window and went down the hall smilin'?"

It took me a second to understand what Jen had said, "You think you saw him after he died?"

"Yes, girl, and didn't you?" Jen saw the surprise on my face, "Never mind, never mind, just forget about it." Jen looked down and held both hands to her face.

"Jen, come on, tell me about this."

"I thought you could see him based on what you said."

"Which was?"

"Somethin' like 'Look at his smile, like he's driftin' away.'"

"But I didn't mean it literally—you can see spirits?"

Jen picked up her coffee cup and explained, "Yes, but I don't usually talk about it because of the way people react—you, for example. I see things other people can't see and my mama warned me not to speak of it."

"Jen, it's okay, I want you to tell me all about it. I can't see spirits, but I believe you." The patients were stirring, call bells were ringing, and the only coffee break that night was cut short.

As I drove out of the hospital parking lot, I saw the rising sun in the rearview mirror. I was too sleepy to fantasize about some silly romance with Alex. Again, and again, my mind replayed the scene of Mr. Allen's death, his smile, and Jen's revelation.

Winter Picnic

The lights flicked off and then on again. The more I focused on the Black Mentalists, the more I was spooked. I couldn't tell whether I was disturbed by my imagination or the actual telepathic influence of these nasty souls.

I had decided over the last few years that Evil—with a capital E—didn't exist. I had this theory, which I thought was profound, that evil was the culmination of mistakes the human race has made trying to become enlightened. My conviction in the nonexistence of evil was being eroded by the last few lessons we were studying. Was it possible that a group of highly evolved souls, overcome with their desire for power, would telepathically try to impede the advancement of others from beyond the grave?

I pulled the granny-square afghan more tightly around my legs. The night was clear and the air was calm. There was no reason for the lights to flicker, but they did. It was midnight. I was awake because of a dream in which I was chased to the edge of a cliff by men in black robes. I tried to settle down by crocheting a doily on which to place a tiny potted jade plant—all my plants had died and I was replacing them one by one.

I heard something fall in the basement. *Did Zane Grey get in again?* I went downstairs and looked around. As I entered the cellar, the lights flicked off again, "Darn it, anyway." I groped my way to the steps and the lights came back on—no cat. I darted up the steps, across the house, and cuddled close to Uriah.

"Watcha' doin', Babe?"

"Checking for Black Mentalists and Boogie Men."

"Find any?"

"They were hiding."

At two-thirty, we were awakened by Zea's screams. Uriah hurried to the kids' room with me following right behind him.

"Don't hurt me. Get away from me!" Zea was thrashing back and forth, sweat beading on her forehead.

"Zea. Wake up. It's okay." Uriah pulled Zea into his arms.

"Get away! Leave me alone."

Zea didn't wake up. I turned on the light.

"Zea. Honey. Wake up." Uriah stroked Zea's hair. "Why isn't she waking up, Alodie?"

"Does she feel warm? Let me check." I felt Zea's forehead and chest. She didn't feel feverish. I took Zea's face in my hands and spoke loudly, "Zea. Wake up!"

Zea opened her eyes and darted looks at me and then Uriah. "Daddy, they were taking me."

"Who was taking you, Sweetie?"

"The monsters."

"You had a bad dream, Zea. You'll be fine now."

Milo was peeking through the fish-shaped hole in the bed Uriah had built for Zea when she was a toddler. The bed sat on the floor like a sand-box and Milo quickly climbed over the side. "Come on, you two. Climb into bed with us and maybe we can sleep through the night without any more bad dreams." I picked up Milo along with his hammer and his blanket. Uriah carried Zea and her doll, Suzie, and we crowded into the double bed and fell asleep.

C3

In the living room, I was winding a grape ivy vine around the strings I had tacked to the trim of the bay window when I saw Uriah drive into the yard. "You're home early," I said, when he entered the room. I leaned in to give him a kiss and he gently pushed me away.

"I don't feel very well—I ache all over."

"Really? It's not like you to get sick." I helped Uriah take off his coat. "You're burning up, Hon."

"Yeah, I know. I had the chills five minutes ago."

"Go to bed and I'll get the thermometer." Uriah flopped onto the bed without taking off his clothes or his boots.

"Shit! One-hundred three degrees. You *are* sick. Let me help you with your boots. I'll get you some water, aspirin and a wet towel. You need to cool down."

"Okay," he said, but didn't move.

"Zea! Come down here. You know you're not supposed to go upstairs anymore. We've closed it off to save heat. Come on."

"No! I want to play in the ladies' room." The small bedroom at the top of the stairs was wallpapered with nineteenth century ladies carrying parasols. It reminded me of the huge painting by George Seurat, "A Sunday Afternoon on the Island of La Grande Jatte." This was a painting I knew well from my childhood trips to the Art Institute in Chicago.

"Please, come down, Zea, all the heat is going upstairs."

"But I have a house set up. All the ladies are walking down the street." Zea had decided she wanted to sleep upstairs in August. The same night her bed and belongings were carried upstairs she changed her mind, claiming she missed Milo and he might be afraid to sleep alone. She used the room instead as a playroom until the cold weather set in.

"Pretend the ladies are walking down the stairs with you."

"I don't want to."

"Zea!"

"No!"

"I'm going to call the Happy Man." I had used this game with the kids with some success. I pretended to call a man, The Happy Man, on the telephone. During a one-way conversation, he suggested I tell the kids they should be nice and cooperate with me. I was the mom after all. The game still worked for Milo, but Zea was getting wise to it.

"Zea." Uriah was out of bed to use the bathroom. He yelled across the house, "Quit arguing with your mom."

"Daddy, I want to play up here and Mommy won't let me."

"Your mom's right, Zea. Come down now!"

"No!"

Uriah, red faced from the fever that hadn't subsided, forced himself to walk across the living room and up the steps. He grabbed Zea by the waist and carried her downstairs.

"I want to stay upstairs!"

"That's enough!" Uriah flipped Zea over his knees and gave her a hefty slap on her butt. "No more arguing." Uriah went back to bed and Zea sat on the floor, stunned.

Through angry tears, she cried, "You can't make me do anything. I'm going back up. You hurt my feelings."

I closed the upstairs door, and stood in front of it. "You just sit where you are and cry by yourself." In a few minutes Zea went into the bedroom mumbling her argument over and over.

Suddenly fatigued, I lay down on the couch to rest for a minute and smelled cat pee. "That darn Zane Grey. Every time she sneaks in, she pees somewhere." Milo was playing with his tinker toys a few feet away. "Milo, you know what? I feel like crap."

"I feel like crap," he repeated. I smiled. He had recently progressed from grunting and mumbling to speaking in well-articulated sentences.

That night, Zea's monsters returned. Uriah didn't wake up. I was glad he was sleeping soundly. I went to comfort Zea who was already awake. "Why do the monsters keep coming after me?"

"Are they the same monsters as last night?"

"Yes, and they chase me. I'm scared. Can I sleep with you?"

"No, Honey. Daddy's sick and I think I'm getting what he has. I'll sit with you until you fall asleep and then I'll leave the light on, okay?" Zea fell asleep half way through the first chapter of *The Yearling*. I went back to bed and fell asleep in minutes.

My next awareness was of floating with my back against the ceiling in the corner of the parlor bedroom. I looked down on the oak desk, the top was painted black. I saw the cradle, outgrown by Milo and now filled with extra pillows and blankets. The old-fashioned pole lamp stood on Uriah's side of the bed. He was flushed with fever. The clock on the night stand read 5:55 a.m. Then, I saw myself sleeping! Consciously, or unconsciously, I'm not sure which, I freaked out and instantly woke up.

"Uriah! I did it. I was out of my body right there above the desk. I saw myself sleeping. I saw you. I saw the clock. It said ... it says 5:56!"

That day, Uriah and I stayed in bed. We were fatigued and achy with fever—it was an effort to move. Zea and Milo were on their own. Zea was given the responsibility to watch Milo, a task she took very seriously. "Mommy and Daddy are sick, so you better be good."

I heard a little more bossing than usual; Zea was in charge. I didn't have the energy to intervene. I took the thermometer out of Uriah's mouth. It still read one-hundred and three. I shook it down, wiped it on the bed sheet and stuck it in my mouth—one hundred and two. "My temp is lower, Uriah. I'll get the kids lunch. I shuffled into the kitchen with the kids hanging onto my pajamas. "Peanut butter and jelly sandwiches and I'll cut up an apple. "Does that sound okay?"

"I don't want …" Zea stopped herself when she saw the exasperation on my face.

"Let's have a picnic in the bedroom," I said. I didn't think I could sit in the kitchen for long.

Zea spread a blanket on the bedroom floor. "There," she said, "a winter picnic in the bedroom."

I lay on Zea's bed and dozed intermittently while the kids played. At five p.m., Uriah came into the room. "My turn," he said, "I'm feeling a little better."

I didn't wake up until eight o'clock the next morning.

"Blue curtains. Blue curtains." Milo pulled on my skirt as I laid sprawled on the stinky couch and stared out the window.

"How did you know I was planning to make blue curtains for these windows?" Now that Milo was talking, he said the weirdest things. My friends at Promise thought he was telepathically gifted.

"Maybe I was talking to myself and decided on blue curtains," I said to Uriah when he came in from feeding the animals. "Maybe Milo heard me. I better be careful what I think about, just in case he can read my thoughts." I ran my fingers through Milo's hair, "I'm glad the kids didn't get sick."

"What was that? I've never been so sick," Uriah wondered.

"Me either. Probably the influenza—it's going around Kankakee, or maybe the Black Mentalists have been messing with us."

"Alodie, you don't believe that."

"Just in case they had anything to do with the flickering lights, the bad dreams, Zea's resistance, and our being sick, no more talk of Black Mentalism. Okay?"

Bumping into Jesus

"Alodie will you run out and get the men while I dish up the pie?" Jen opened a kitchen drawer and dug through the utensils. "I think they're in the garage."

Jen and I had finally managed to get our families together for a visit. Our separate and complicated lives left little overlapping free time. Dinner and dishes were finished, and we were ready to relax and have dessert. Lee, Jen's husband, and Uriah skipped out on clean-up because Lee was anxious to show Uriah the "elephant pistol" he had built by welding a short pipe onto a conglomeration of gun parts. He hadn't shot the thing yet for fear it might backfire into his face or blow off his arm.

As different in appearance as they were in background, the two men shared an interest in the unusual. Lee had dark brown nappy hair, black eyes and bronze skin—he came from African/Irish roots. He was raised by his grandparents in the village of Pembroke, ten miles east of Kankakee and, although poor, he spoke light-heartedly of his childhood. In contrast, Uriah had wavy, white-blond hair, blue diamond eyes, and skin so fair the pink showed through from underneath. He descended from Dutch immigrants. His father became affluent buying and selling land on the southern edge of Chicago. He was dominating and sometimes emotionally oppressive.

Uriah brought his guitar along as Jen had requested. "Darlin,' do you know that moon song?"

"Moon song?" Uriah closed his eyes and scanned his memory.

"Cat Stevens sings it," Lee offered a clue.

"Moon Shadow?"

"Yes, that's it." Jen started singing before Uriah could strike a chord. "'I'm being followed by a moon shadow' . . ." I joined in.

"Wait a minute, hold it," Uriah said, as he tried to establish a key.

We sang on, "'If I ever lose my mouth, all my teeth north and south.'"

Lee lit a cigarette and stood in the door frame. With our combined effort, Jen, Uriah and I recalled all the verses.

"Speaking of shadows, Jen, did you ever get that ghost out of your house?" Uriah had been waiting all evening to ask.

I leaned forward in my chair in anticipation of a good story, "Is he still here?"

"Nope," Lee answered in his low silky voice. "She irritated him so much, old George high-tailed out of here."

Jen settled back into the overstuffed sectional. "At first, I tried to reason with the man. I said, 'You're dead, and this isn't your house anymore. We bought this trailer and moved it here. It's crowded enough without some drifter hangin' 'round. I went on and on at him every time I'd see him, but he didn't leave. Then, I remembered that in Saint Thomas, folks hang stuff around the house after somebody dies to encourage the spirits to go wherever they're supposed to go. So, I did that."

"You should have smelled the place," Lee added, "garlic all over, and she hung crosses everywhere. I couldn't go through a door without bumping into Jesus."

"I thought what I did must have worked because I didn't see George for about a week. Then, last Sunday, I took a nap. Remember how busy it was at work, Alodie? I rolled over to get comfortable and there he was, right next to the bed. He scared the dickens out of me. I was so angry I started yellin' at him. I got right out of bed and said, 'You get out of here! Get on with it. You're dead. Go do what dead people do.' I chased him right out the door and he hasn't come back."

"Do you think he's gone for good?" Uriah asked.

"I think so. It feels like he took himself and his trouble with him." Jen stood up and went into the kitchen, "Anyone want coffee?"

"Jen, do you see spirits all over the place?" I asked, unsatiated. I spoke a little louder so Jen could hear over the running water.

"Oh, no, Hon, only once in a while. I ran into one the other day comin' 'round the corner in front of the Kankakee court house. I don't like the feelin'—it's sort of like walking through cobwebs. The sensation sticks with me for a long time."

"Have you ever heard of astral travel?" I asked. Jen and Lee shook their heads. "At Promise, people try to leave their bodies or use a different one—an energy body."

Jen nodded her head in recognition. "Oh, sure, you're talkin' 'bout floatin' around when you're sleeping. I do that sometimes."

"Now, Jenavieve."

Uriah didn't notice Lee's unease. "Do you do it on purpose?"

"Not usually. I just wake up and find myself floatin' on the ceiling"

"You do not, come on, Jen."

"I do so, Lee. I'll prove it to you sometime," Jen winked at him. "Let's sing some more. How about, *When the Saints Come Marching In?*"

"You're kidding, right?" Lee lit up another cigarette.

"Those are gonna kill him someday, but he won't quit."

Uriah, still in an other-worldly state of mind, began singing, "'Farther along, we'll know more about it. Farther along, we'll understand why.'"

I joined in with a harmony, "'Cheer up, my brother. Live in the sunshine. We'll understand it all by and by.'"

White Lines

"This just ticks me off. Look at this Uriah. Brown polyester stretch pants and a gold blouse to match, also polyester, I might add. And, isn't this beautiful? The grandest piece of gold crap you could ever hang around your neck. I would never wear a necklace like this, and my mom knows it. She just won't give up. She won't let me live my own life. I'm not keeping any of this and I'm going to call Mom and tell her I'm sending back my entire birthday present."

I was crazy mad. Uriah watched and listened as I ranted, but he looked surprised when I dialed the phone. "Mom, when will you stop trying to make me into someone I'm not? I don't care if all the young girls are wearing clothes like these. I will never wear them … I don't believe in your religion either … No, we're not coming home for Thanksgiving. We're not coming home again until you decide to let me live my own life. I do mean it. Goodbye."

I took a dive onto the couch. "I can't believe I just did that. Jesus! I'm so tired of the 'better than thou' attitude I grew up with and that arrogant asshole minister. And all mom's bizarre accusations; I think she's a little schizy. I'm still mad at her for saying I made it with the guy down the street."

"Take it easy, Alodie, that happened years ago."

"I want to punch something."

During the next several days, I was an emotional wreck. I fretted and fumed—guilt see-sawed with self-righteousness. I tried not to burden Uriah with repetitive complaining.

CR

Uriah answered the phone during supper in the middle of December. I didn't get the gist of the conversation and when he hung up, he said, "That was someone from Promise—I didn't recognize the name. Beatrice has moved to Wisconsin with a group of her faithful and a special meeting has been planned for tomorrow night to discuss what we should do. I'm supposed to call a few other people to let them know. Eve and Hans are going to watch the kids in the basement of the school."

"Maybe we'll go from a monarchy to an oligarchy by default," I said.

"You mean the core group? How many of them are likely to stay?"

"What about Victor? Does he have any clout anymore?"

"He's not officially back in the group," Uriah said, "not according to Hermie anyway."

"Rita said people have seen Victor sneaking around. He led the public meeting in Chicago last month. Maybe it's about time Promise became a democracy. Most of us are totally ignorant about what's going on. You work your butt off and we've completely changed our lifestyles for the cause, if you can call it that. Maybe the group will just implode."

"Just relax, will you, Alodie? Maybe we'll find out what's going on tomorrow night."

"Or not."

The conversation diverged. "I guess I'll have to make two trips into Promise tomorrow—it's a school day for Zea. I hope the weather cooperates." I framed my face in my hands against the window. "The stars are bright, Uriah, there's a ring around the moon."

"When you're gone tomorrow, maybe I'll butcher rabbits. I don't like to do it when the kids are around, actually, I don't like to do it at all. When those bunnies squeal it makes me queasy. I might become a vegetarian for a while. The fast we did was easy enough and not eating meat should be easier than that."

"The fast helped my legs, that's for sure, but it was only for two days. I'm not going to be a vegetarian. Are you serious? I'd miss a good burger now and then, and I think animal protein is good for the kids."

"We'll see. It's just a thought."

The lights of Promise arose in the distance from the black fields. The original farmhouse, the barn and out-buildings, stood in contrast to the new homes and factories. "These houses seem extravagant," I said.

"They're not though, Alodie, they're practical. They look big because they are built on slabs. They're well insulated and earthquake proof."

"Maybe, I don't know, it just doesn't appeal to me to live in a subdivision like this. The idea of Prosperity Consciousness bothers me. There's a fine line between prosperity and blatant materialism." I struggled with this tenet of the group which I interpreted to mean—if you believe you're prosperous and act like your prosperous, you'll become prosperous.

"You're so cheap, Alodie. You don't spend a dime, if you can spend a nickel."

"Well, yeah."

"Maybe the dime will buy you something that lasts a little longer."

"What if you only have a nickel?"

Uriah parked in front of the school and we brought the kids inside. Eve said, "We plan to stay overnight with the kids who live here at Promise. You're welcome to leave Zea and Milo if you want to."

"It depends how late the meeting gets and on the weather," I said, we're supposed to have some snow tonight."

Hans showed Milo the toy trucks, and while he was thoroughly engaged, we ducked out. Milo usually squalled when we left him with a sitter.

The meeting was in the wood-working factory on the edge of the neighborhood. We were joined by friends as we walked toward the building. "The next chapter in the saga of Promise," Rita said. No one replied. Promise remained serious business because it was a huge commitment for most of us.

Alex slipped behind Rita, then behind Uriah and me. He tugged on the bottom edge of my coat and I turned around, "Hey, Alex." He winked in reply.

William called the meeting to order through the din of anticipation. "It is true," he began. "As you can see by their absence, several members of the group joined Beatrice and moved to northwestern Wisconsin. The reason for this separation stems from many problems that have plagued the group over the years. In the absence of Victor, Beatrice, and most of the original core group, we need to establish a new system of government."

There was a low hum in response. William continued, "The Brotherhood intended the Kingdom of God to be a democracy and I believe the departure of Victor and Beatrice is a sign we are ready to govern ourselves." There was another low rumble that matched the wind whipping against the aluminum siding. A cheer started slowly, and then built into a standing show of approval.

William waited until the group settled. "There are many legal problems we'll have to solve, especially in regard to the ownership of the property."

"Someone shouted from the side of the room, "Maybe we should elect officers." Another rumble, this time of differing opinions.

"A strong people need no leader!"

"But how are we going to get organized?"

"I say we nominate a temporary president. I nominated William."

"I second it."

William tried to bring the meeting back to order, "Let's slow down a little. We don't have to decide anything tonight. Let's give it a week. In the meantime, consider how you would like Promise to be structured. How should property be owned? How should new members be screened and accepted? Who should be allowed to vote? Think about the universal laws and how we can apply them."

The group agreed to adjourn and think—there was no rush to make these big decisions. The shock of what William said hung in the air and people lingered.

"What kind of problems have plagued the community for years?" Uriah asked.

"Infidelity," Alex said.

"Whose infidelity?" I didn't take time to think.

"Victor's?" Hermie, Uriah and Rita questioned in unison.

"Alex, is that right?" I didn't want to believe it.

"You got it."

"Alex, how do you know?" Rita asked, doubtfully. "Why didn't you tell me? I can't believe you would keep a secret like that."

"I overheard an argument between Beatrice and Victor when I was installing a new phone line in the office. It seemed like destructive information, so I kept it to myself."

"And it isn't destructive now?"

"Circumstances have changed."

It was after midnight when Uriah and I left the meeting. Little pebbles of snow were scooting over the sidewalk and biting at our cheeks. "Should we leave the kids?" I answered my own question. "Let's just check on them and if Milo's asleep, we can pick them up first thing tomorrow."

"I'll go," Uriah said. "Why don't you start the car." I saw Uriah's beret blow away in the wind as he opened the door to the school.

I walked past a long line of cars parked on the edge of the curved street. I concentrated on my footing and held a scarf over my face. An arm reached around my shoulders and startled me. "Alex. Shit."

"A little jumpy, aren't you?"

"Yeah, I can't see a darn thing and we're gonna try to drive home."

"Rita wants to stay with someone in Promise. She's asking around."

"Probably wise. We're going to leave the kids but Uriah thinks we can make it."

"You don't have quite as far to go as we do. Hey, give me a hug. This night was so weird."

Two miles west of Promise, Uriah turned north. "It's hard to see driving straight into the wind," he said, as he flipped the headlights from dim to bright and back to dim. "It doesn't make any difference. I can't see anything."

I stared into the snow. "This reminds me of the last scene from *2001: A Space Odyssey*."

"How would you know? You fell asleep."

"Yeah, but I remember the last scene when the spaceship goes at light speed through the stars. Watch out, Uriah!" I gasped as he drove onto the shoulder.

"That helps a lot."

"You scared me."

"I really can't see where I'm going and the drifts are getting deeper. Maybe we should turn back."

"That doesn't make sense, we're half-way home. It's not safe to stop, it's below zero. Let's keep going. If we have to, we can stop at a farm somewhere."

"If we can even see a yard light."

I tried to see the center line or the white line along the shoulder, but I could see nothing. "Maybe, if I open the car door, I can see the line on the edge of the road."

"You can try it, but it's gonna be cold."

I opened the door and looked down. The car blocked the wind enough for me to see the white line. The hard-packed drifts were deepening, but we were still able to plow through them. "A little left, good. Right—not so much." For forty-five minutes I guided Uriah as he crept the next three miles into the little town of Cabery.

"We can't go on," Uriah said, "We have to stop."

"Where, Uriah? Like Cabery has a gas station or a motel? We don't know anybody here."

"I do know a couple of guys. They live on the corner of the crossroads. They were at the meeting tonight and maybe they made it home already. Otherwise, we'll have to knock on a stranger's door."

The wind was broken by the houses in town and Uriah pulled to the side of the road as he neared the corner. "There it is," he said. "Over there. The lights are still on."

Uriah and I trudged through the yard. "Skirts are so stupid!" I complained, as the snow stung my shins. "I guess I should have worn something underneath."

One of the men was still awake and he graciously made a bed for me on the couch and one for Uriah on the floor.

"I hope this is all right," he said.

"It's great," I said. "You saved us."

After the lights were out, I was unable to relax. My nerves were frazzled by the sound of the wind and the visual imprint of the snow hitting the windshield. I reached down for Uriah's hand. "I love you, Hon."

"Love you too."

As usual, I had trouble sleeping away from home and was awake for what seemed like hours. I thought about Alex. As attracted as I was to him, he was starting to irritate me. What was it? Were we back in high school? He was hovering. My thoughts looped around and around between Alex and Promise. Should we stick with Promise? The community was falling apart. Then, I began reciting the Universal Lemurian Laws—the Constitution of the Kingdom of God.

One: No one may profit at the expense of another.

Two: No one, nor any government, may take anything from a person or another nation by force.

Three: Natural resources shall belong to the commonwealth of all citizens and shall not be owned by any person or corporation of persons.

Four: Every citizen is due equal education and the freedom to choose a vocation, and has equal rights before the law.

Five: All promotions shall be based upon personal merit and proficiency.

Six: Everyone must compensate fully for every personal possession they receive and hope to retain.

Seven: No person, nor the government, may operate in the environment of another, unless specifically requested to do so by that person. The government, however, may enforce the law in treasonable, criminal, and civil suits.

Eight: No one may kill or injure another except in defense of his life or state.

Nine: The sanctity of the home is inviolate, except if there is a threat to life within the home.

Ten: If no violation of the above law is involved, the majority rule will apply and be subject to the approval of the Brotherhood's direct representatives whose decisions will be final.

Every time I recited the Lemurian Laws, I thought about how I would like to tweak them. I wasn't sure about treason or civil suits and I didn't like the idea of killing someone in defense of the state. Since I had no empirical evidence of the Brotherhood's existence, I didn't think they should have the final say. Why have a democracy at all? It sounded like the electoral college or even a dictatorship. Who exactly was the Brotherhood's direct representative, Victor? But, aside from these questions, the Lemurian Laws were brilliant. If we could live by them and the Great Virtues, we would live in a Utopia. I would be happy with that.

Floating in From Fourth

had told the night supervisor I would float to other units, if necessary. It was another reason I felt anxious when I arrived at work. I was never sure where I would end up. The experience would be good for my career in the long run, but scary at the moment. Adaptability wasn't one of the Great Virtues, but I thought it was important.

When I entered the fourth-floor conference room for the shift report, I wasn't surprised to be asked to go to pediatrics. The nurse who usually worked peds would be in charge. This news eased my fluttering stomach, and I hurried downstairs to catch as much as I could of the evening report.

I could feel a greater level of excitement than usual as I slipped into the meeting. The nurses acknowledged my entrance with only a swift glance.

"I'm afraid to go in there," the evening nurse said. "They all give me the creeps. It's no wonder the kid's having seizures. He's probably scared out of his wits."

"Seizures aren't caused from being scared," the night nurse, Alice, skewed one side of her face and shook her head.

"What else is interesting, is that Joey, that's the kids name, had a perfectly normal EEG in the ER."

"Hmm, that's a little weird," Alice said. "If his seizures are atypical and as severe as you say, there should be some evidence on the EEG."

"Yeah, you'd think."

Both nurses looked at me.

"I'm Alodie, floating in from fourth."

"Great, we're gonna need the extra help tonight. You've got to hear about this case."

"Hey, wait," the evening nurse complained, "Could we finish report so I can do my charting and get home sometime tonight?"

Beside the boy with the seizures, there were two kids with asthma, one with pneumonia, a girl with a badly broken leg and a baby who had just returned from neonatal intensive care after a repair of a pyloric stenosis. She would need close observation. She was being fed with a tube until the connections between her esophagus and stomach healed.

"Anyway," Alice resumed after the evening nurse left the room, "Joey's parents are Satanists."

I raised my eyebrows.

"Really. There are like six people in the room all dressed in black. They're wearing weird jewelry and are tattooed with strange symbols and shit. They've been chanting and working spells over the kid all evening and that's why no one wants to go in there. The lights are out and there are about twenty candles burning, even though candles aren't allowed in the hospital. The supervisor and security told them so, but they got belligerent and said it was their religious right."

"We'll have to go in eventually," I said. "Let's check on the other kids and then go in together."

The nursing assistant approached excitedly, "Those people in thirty-three are scary and I'm not going in there again."

I passed the lounge where two men and two women, all wearing black robes, talked quietly together. Alice and I finished our rounds. I knocked on the door of room thirty-three.

There was no reply from within so I cracked the door. "Hello, I'm Alodie, the nurse." The room was dark and it took a few seconds for my eyes to adjust.

Alice came in behind me. "I'm Alice," she said. The bed was pulled away from the wall—one person sat at the head and another at the foot.

I walked to the edge of the bed. Joey's eyes were closed, but I greeted him anyway. "Hi, Joey, I'm Alodie. Alice is with me." I saw Joey peek from one eye. "We'll be taking care of you tonight. Are these you're parents?" The woman at the head of the bed nodded.

"Joey, are you awake? Can you squeeze my hands?" Alice asked. Joey squeezed. "Good. Since you're awake, I want to look at your eyes with a flashlight to see how well your pupils respond to the light."

"No, you will not," said Joey's mother. "That is totally unnecessary."

Alice lowered her voice and said with impressive authority, "He's in the hospital for observation and that is what we intend to do, Mrs. Duncan."

"It's not with my approval. The school called the ambulance, and here he is. We agreed to observation tonight, but we're taking him home in the morning."

"Can I get you anything, Joey?" I asked. He stirred slightly and suddenly stiffened his neck. "He's gonna seize, Alice." I squeezed around the head of the bed, pushing back Joey's mom. Alice and I held our arms across Joey to prevent him from injury. His parents began rocking back and forth with their hands stretched over his head and feet. They mumbled and chanted nonsensical syllables. We waited until the seizure subsided and left the room.

"That was a weird seizure, wasn't it?" I asked. "The spasms were symmetrical and he didn't arch his back at all—he didn't hold his breath either."

"Gosh," Alice considered "I didn't really notice. I was freaked out by the parents."

"And, he just happened to have a seizure while we were standing next to him."

"You think he's faking?"

"Possibly. Let's finish our treatments and I'll study the chart to see if there is a pattern to the times and descriptions of the seizures he had today."

At two o'clock, I went to the fourth floor to get my lunch from my locker. Jen came out of the supply room. "Jen!" I grabbed her arm. "We have a strange situation downstairs. Do you think there is anything to the Satanic stuff that's been on the news?"

"No, I don't think so—it's just a fad."

I told Jen about Joey.

"Do you want me to come downstairs, Darlin', to see what I see?"

"Would you?"

"I'll try to come in an hour or so."

Alice and I were setting up medications for morning rounds when Jen burst into the room. "Jesus, bless us all," she shuddered.

"What is it? What's the matter?"

"I went into that child's room."

"By yourself?"

"It was on the way. When you go in there again, turn on all the lights, make as much noise as you can. Bang on bedpans if you need, and don't go in alone. There are spirits everywhere, even in the hallway, and they don't seem happy."

Alice hadn't blinked for over a minute. "I'll explain later," I said. Jen, in her excitement, hadn't considered Alice's possible reaction.

"Be really careful. Remember, turn on the lights and don't leave the child alone if you can help it, at least not for long. Check on him as often as you can."

Jen left and Alice said, "I'm freaking out here, Alodie, what was that all about?"

"Jen says she can see spirits."

"Come on, Alodie."

"I know it sounds crazy. We saw a death together and she saw the man's spirit leave. Jen thought I could see it too."

"Could you?"

"No."

"What if Jen's right? What are we supposed to do now? Call the supervisor and tell her Joey shouldn't be left alone because there are ghosts in his room? We don't have the staff to cover one-on-one."

I realized how absurd the story would—did sound. "We could tell her we think Joey is afraid of his parents and he might be faking his seizures."

"That, we could do, I'll call her."

"Maybe we could get the orderly to hang out with Joey. I'll get some utensils together to rattle around when we go in the room." Alice rolled her eyes. "Just in case," I said.

The night supervisor sent the orderly. Joey's parents came to the desk several times to protest, but Alice stood firm. "We think Joey is afraid," she said, "and until we know what's happening, we're going to stay with him. You can take your complaints to the doctor in the morning."

"I certainly will!" Joey's mom wailed. "And that's not all I'll do."

We discussed the night's events with the supervisor prior to report. "Do you think we should call social services? This seems like child abuse."

"But what if he is having real seizures?"

"Maybe they gave him a magic potion that made him sick," the nursing assistant suggested.

"Hadn't thought of that."

The supervisor said, "I'll call the doctor right away. Could you girls stay until she gets here and describe the situation? Good work, by the way."

"Thanks."

A few minutes later, Alice asked me if we should tell the doctor about the ghosts.

"She'll think we're as crazy as the Satanists; we should probably stick to the facts."

"Probably," Alice agreed.

The road home seemed endless. I was exhausted. I didn't know what I believed or what I felt about what had happened. I wanted to believe in ghosts and I wanted to believe Jen was psychic—that she was telling the truth and not just a little crazy. I wanted to believe in everything I was learning at Promise. I wanted to believe and I wanted to see what Jen could see.

Let It Be

"I'm not sure what I should do," I said to Uriah's mother, as I helped her put away the groceries on the Saturday before Christmas.

"You're the one who decided not to see your mom anymore," she said, "and you're the one who will need to fix it."

"I know you're right, but it's so hard."

"You need to decide what kind of relationship you're going to have with her. Maybe you need to accept her viewpoint if you want her to accept yours."

"I suppose, although acceptance is probably beyond my capability. Tolerance might work."

"It's worth the effort, isn't it?" Uriah's mother, usually reticent, had a definite opinion about my problem with my mom.

"I don't want to alienate my kids from her, they should know both of their grandmas."

"Yes, they should."

I knew there was no easy fix to the mess I had made with my mom, "I'll have to apologize somehow."

Christmas with Uriah's family was ... what? Overwhelming? There were seven siblings, plus in-laws, nieces and nephews and I loved it. I only had a brother and a sister who were just starting their families. This party was fun, but there was a lingering sadness because this was only the second Christmas after Uriah's dad had died.

I called Jen the next morning. "Hey, Jen, we're on our way home from Uriah's mom's and we thought we would stop to see you, if that's okay."

"Uriah," I said, as we began the drive, "I think we should have another baby."

"Really? You're ready?"

Zea overheard, "Are we gonna have another baby?"

"Maybe later, Zea."

"We talked about having three kids."

"Let's think about it. What brought this on??

I love your big family and I think we should have more kids. I worry about it sometimes because of the miscarriage."

"But that was almost a year before Milo was born."

"I know, but I worry, you know how I worry."

"What's a miscarriage?" Zea asked.

"I'll tell you about it later, Honey."

We were quiet for a while. I was remembering the miscarriage—I suppose Uriah was too.

As we drove into the mostly black, rural community on the sandy flats east of the Kankakee River, I attributed my uneasiness to unfamiliarity. The gate was locked on the cyclone fence surrounding Jen and Lee's yard and Uriah had to shout to get Lee's attention. Their mobile home was set back behind his grandparent's cement block house.

"How y'all doin'?" he asked, shaking Uriah's hand after he released the padlock on the gate. "Alodie, you take the kids on in. I'm gonna have a smoke and feed the turtles." Lee offered Uriah a cigarette and I flashed Uriah a disapproving eye as he pulled a cigarette from Lee's pack. He was breaking the rules—not that I disapproved of bumming a cigarette now and then. I thought Uriah's philosophy of 'all things in moderation' made more sense than the absolutism of Promise. He tossed a teasing look right back at me.

I guided Zea and Milo through the snow along the narrowly shoveled path to the door. "Merry Christmas, Darlin's," Jen hugged all three of us at once.

It took us a few minutes to unbundle and then I asked, "Jen, Lee was talking about feeding the turtles, what's that about?"

"Lee caught a couple of snapping turtles last fall. He filled up the old cistern and keeps 'em down there—he feeds 'em hamburger."

I looked out the window. "They're huge! Zea. Milo. Look!" I lifted Milo to the window as Zea squeezed in next to him to watch the snapping turtles devour raw hamburger along with mouthfuls of blood-stained snow.

After a dinner of chicken, ham and sweet potatoes, I told Jen and Lee that I had floated out of my body when Uriah and I were sick. I knew I could safely tell Jen about my weird experience.

"I told you, Alodie, that I float around too sometimes," Jen said.

Lee said, "Jen, tell them about your little experiment."

"He doesn't believe me, so I planned to prove it. I told him that while I was sleepin' in the afternoon I would look for him and tell him what I saw him doin'. I told him to lock me in the house. Around two o'clock I woke up, well, not really, but I started floatin' and lookin' for Lee. I didn't find him inside, so I drifted through the door and found him tinkering on a motor in the garage. I wanted to get back to the house to wake up and tell him, but I couldn't figure out how to get in because the door was locked. I started to panic and woke up."

"You didn't need to use the door, did you?" Uriah wondered.

"No, but when you're travelin' without your brain, you get a little mixed up."

"Cool. Lee, did she know what you were doing in the garage?"

"Yeah, but I fool with that motor every day and she could have guessed that." He went outside for a smoke.

"Jen, do you *try* to float out of your body?"

"I can do it on purpose, but usually it just happens."

"Do you do it a lot?"

"Oh, no, I don't think it's particularly useful."

While the dishes were being washed and put away the conversation drifted back to work, babies, families and holidays.

"I agree with Uriah's mama about you gettin' yourself home for Christmas. You need to stay connected with your family, otherwise you'll feel a sadness inside that will never go away."

"You're right, I know you're right."

"Let it be," Jen said. "You can't change people, Alodie. There's a song about that!" She laughed and we began to sing. "When I find myself in times of trouble . . ."

Arrogance

cicles as tall as Zea hung from the eaves of the farmhouse roof. The snow had melted enough to reveal an accumulation of silt lifted from the plowed fields by the horizontal winds of winter. The day was warm enough for an adventure and as I pulled the bedspread into place, I glanced at the lone hill that stood about a mile to the west.

Coal mines had peppered the area one hundred years before. The evidence left behind were eroding slag hills, boom towns reclaimed by nature, and the eerie feeling of interloping souls.

"Zea, would you like to walk to the ghost town and see if we can climb the mound?"

The answer was a quick, "Yes." Milo zoomed to the door.

Pushing Milo in his blue vinyl stroller along the muddy gravel road was arduous, especially when Zea insisted riding piggyback on the rear axle. If I had allowed Milo to toddle along, the hike would have taken even longer.

The jogging, yoga and the weekend fast had relieved the ache in my legs and the lightness in my step felt wonderful—I was myself again. As we bumped along, Zea and Milo experimented with the involuntary vibrato of their voices.

"This must be where the town started," I said, "See, there are old sidewalks here." Grass, weeds and moss had carpeted the heaved and broken concrete.

"There's an old chimney, Mommy." Zea had picked up on my enthusiasm and we pretended to be archeologists. Smoke from a down-draft burned our eyes and noses as we turned north on the only street still in use in the once vital town. The smoke came from a stove pipe wired in slipshod fashion to the ridge of a roof on a typical prairie town general store. The building had a gable roof with a false front and a transom window above the door. The show windows reached from floor to ceiling—the fancy trim was weathered and broken.

I hoped not to be seen by the elderly woman who lived in the place and we slipped quickly past on the far side of the street. Uriah's friend, Joe, had a penchant for odd people and places. On a Sunday afternoon drive he had discovered the town and the woman. He thought she was a novelty.

We had given our attack rooster, Spurs, to Joe. We had had to carry a stick with us when we went into the chicken house and were afraid he might hurt the kids. Joe got so mad at Spurs, he blew him up with a shot gun. Uriah thought that was a waste of a pot of good chicken soup. There was something hidden in Joe—something he wouldn't, or couldn't, disclose. He had described his mother as "odd" and said she once threw a knife at his dad. He didn't quite fit in at Promise, he was a loner, perhaps from a different socioeconomic class than most of the members, but we never discussed his background. What we knew were the tidbits he offered.

A month earlier, Joe had convinced us to go with him to visit his eccentric new friend. The evening was a blur. I had been bored and uncomfortable chatting about what? Joe and the woman were on the same page—I was in a different book. The visual was of an old, but not ancient woman, smoking a pipe, smelling like vanilla and a moldy basement. The two young men who sat in the corners spooked me because they didn't say a word. The woman probably had a fascinating immigrant miner's daughter heritage—that would interest me, but I couldn't squeeze in the question. I could relate to the braided rugs she made from discarded wool suits and silk ties, but I couldn't relate to talk for talk's sake. Uriah accused me of the same, but my chatter was never meaningless.

I wasn't curious about quirky people, at least not while they were still living. I preferred to focus my curiosity on the non-human oddities of nature, of science, which didn't threaten my identity. I don't know if my identity was fragile or if I was just impatient with behavior I didn't understand. What was the saying? I didn't suffer fools. I was being arrogant and arrogance was certainly not a Great Virtue.

The coal mine was not like the ones Uriah and I had visited near Braidwood. It was an underground mine, not an open pit. There were no depressions or ponds anywhere around this mound. Concentric circles of barbed wire discouraged visitors from approaching. Although not able to get within one-hundred feet of the bottom of the hill, I could read the "No Trespassing/Danger" sign nailed to boards barring the entrance into the mine. I wasn't one to break safety rules, especially not the dictates of a sign—unlike Uriah, who often considered a rule to be a personal challenge. I turned around and endured Milo's protest on the journey home. He was angry because he couldn't climb the forbidden hill.

"I hear a baby crying," Zea shouted through the back door which I had pried open to let in the earthy smell of spring. In the next breath, Zea said, "Come and see my rivers and dams, Mommy."

"What did you say about a baby crying, Zea?"

"There is a baby crying in the chicken coop."

"That can't be, Zea." Then I heard the sound Zea had interpreted as the sound of a baby's cry and it did sound strangely so. "We better check it out."

We slogged through compact drifts of waterlogged snow and rounded the chicken coop. Along the south wall sat an animal; it's hip bones and ribs protruded through wet gray fur and its head was stuck in a tin can. "Oh, Mommy," Zea cried, "It's Zane Grey!"

Zea was right. Zane Grey had been missing for several days, perhaps a week, and here she was, stumbling blindly about in the melting snow. I felt a cringe of guilt. I had punctured open several tin cans with an old-fashioned can opener/bottle opener. The cat must have looked for a treat among the discarded cans, slid her head into one, but couldn't pull it out against the sharp inwardly turned edge.

I took Zane Grey, head in can, to the house. With tinsnips, I cut and spread the rusty metal and released the pitiful creature.

Uriah came in from chores the next morning noticeably quiet. He opened a couple of kitchen cabinets and took out a bowl and a box of Cheerios.

"What's going on, Uriah?"

"I turned the chickens and the rabbits loose."

We had talked about freeing the animals, but still hadn't decided if we should. I looked into the backyard. The filthy chickens, which had been caged in cubicles since they were old enough to lay eggs, were tearing around under the apple trees, scratching and clucking in celebration. "They seem happier than you do."

"I don't know if it was the right thing to do. I know we won't get as many eggs—at least we won't be able to find them and the rabbits will probably run away.

"So why did you do it?"

"Because I don't want the animals to live in such dismal conditions. I can't kill another rabbit. I'm going vegetarian for a while."

"That's gonna be a hassle for me, Uriah, I hate to cook anyway. I'll have to make different food for you, or maybe you can just make your own."

"Don't get mad, Alodie, just make what you always do and cook the meat separately."

"I can do that, I guess, but could you start after tonight? I bought a leg of lamb for Passover."

"Sure, why not?" Uriah went to the refrigerator for milk and noticed something through the north window. "Looks like we're in for a visit from your favorite neighbors."

"Not again!"

"I wonder if Wayne got his transmission fixed."

"Why? What's the deal with that?"

"His car doesn't have reverse."

"What do they want to borrow this time?" Even though during the last weeks of the winter I had an acute case of cabin fever, I had not relished the almost daily visits from Tammy and her three lousy, snot-nosed, timorous girls. I deliberately hardened my heart against the sunken eyes and pallor of the children—they were malnourished. Tammy's demeanor and negative comments were classic symptoms of depression, but I didn't want to take on the revivification of this family. They had made their own decision to squat in an abandoned house with no electricity. It was crawling with cockroaches, and was seriously too cold for comfort. It was a decision I never would have made. What was I supposed to do? Let them move in with us? Wouldn't that be grand? I rationalized my lack of kindness every time I saw Tammy trudge down the gravel road to visit.

"Would you like a cup of coffee?" Uriah asked, "Did you have breakfast?"

I correctly anticipated the answers.

Uriah made a big pot of oatmeal, and after devouring several helpings Wayne explained, in excruciating detail, that he had found a job at the feed mill in Dwight. One of the bosses knew of a trailer he and Tammy could stay in for free until he could save a little money. Tammy and Wayne had come over to say goodbye and thank us for our help—a feeling of guilt began to suffocate me.

That evening, I set the table for five as beautifully as our hodgepodge of dishes would allow. The matching plates and silverware were symmetrically arranged and the hand-me-down square stemmed wine glasses were glimmering. The extra place setting at the head of the table was for the prophet Elijah, in case he dropped by. This was the first time Uriah and I celebrated Passover. The people of Promise, even though mostly of Christian background, observed Seder because of Victor's conviction that the major holidays of all religions should be honored. Passover was especially important because it celebrated the freeing of an oppressed people.

All afternoon, Uriah and I told Zea and Milo—as much as he cared to listen—the story of the Israelite's captivity in Egypt, of Pharaoh, the plagues, and Moses parting the Red Sea. I rehearsed with Zea the answers to "The Questions for the Child," so she could answer them during the reading of the Haggadah. We had made matzoth and had gathered dandelion greens to mix with horseradish for the bitter herbs. We chopped apples and nuts to symbolize the mortar made by the Israelites and the yummy smell of roasting lamb filled the house.

While I was lighting the candles on the table, the phone rang. Uriah answered it in the kitchen. He returned to the table with an expression I couldn't read and it sent me into a panic. "What's wrong? What happened?"

"We have to move." he said slowly. "The landlord's son wants to live here."

"Shit. How long do we have?"

"Three weeks."

I was so content. I loved living in the country. I loved our house and I loved the friends we had made at Promise. My gloom about harshly judging Tammy and Wayne returned. "It's easy to blame people for making bad decisions," I said.

Uriah looked surprised, "I don't think we made any bad decisions."

"Maybe the landlord didn't like us having a calf and chicks in the basement."

Part 2

Potential

I counted three layers of linoleum curled up along the walls of the kitchen. My eyes followed the wall up to the water-stained wallpaper and the exposed plaster lath on the ceiling.

"You won't find a better deal on a fixer-upper," the realtor explained to Uriah in the next room. My glance fell quickly to the floor as I tripped over the threshold between rooms. A thick-midriffed grey-haired woman didn't look up from her ironing when I pulled away a blanket hanging in the doorway of a back room and peeked inside. As I continued through the house following the men, the floors swelled and fell like waves. The window shades and curtains were pulled down throughout the house—the dim light served the realtor's purpose.

The original house, from what I could determine, was a two-room, two story, front to back pioneer homestead. The expansion of the house was sequential, one room added on and then another around the perimeter—all the rooms were connected.

I had made a decision, based on the condition of the kitchen, that this place was a dump and we were not going to buy it.

"You can't beat it for $11,000," the realtor said. The men crossed the front porch and walked into the driveway.

I hurried to join them, grabbed Uriah by the elbow and dragged him into the back yard.

"Uriah, we can't buy this house. It's a mess. It's falling apart!"

"It has potential."

"Let's look at some other places."

"We have, Alodie, this is the best deal we'll find. We can fix it up and sell it for a profit."

"But we'll have to live in it in the meantime."

"It will be fun—like camping out."

"I don't want to camp out," I said, but I could feel myself giving in. Uriah could usually convince me to do anything. I had veto power, but I rarely exercised it. Why? I'm too fricking easy, I hate conflict and Uriah loves a challenge. He's confident and I'm a wuss. "At least get the realtor to come down on the price. What are we going to do for a down payment?"

"We'll get a construction loan." Uriah was impulsive, but his impulsiveness and his creativity were combined. He could see the end result. He had already redesigned and rebuilt the house in his imagination and I knew he was capable and determined.

"I'll see if I can make a deal."

While Uriah and the realtor looked at the outside of the house, I poked my head into a Quonset shed on the side boundary of the property. There were a few usable treasures inside—including two oak chairs. I sat down on one of them and looked at the blooming periwinkle that bordered a scrubby tangle of brush and trees on the edge of the back yard. I fought my way through the brush to a muddy creek. The smell of budding cottonwood and damp earth mingled with the smell of sewage. I walked back to the house surveying the yard and planned a long narrow vegetable garden along the north boundary. The wood-grain asphalt siding on the house caught my attention; there was little redeemable about the place.

I heard Uriah lower his voice and tell the realtor, business-like, "There are structural problems, see that flat valley between the kitchen and the bathroom? It must have four inches of tar on it, and it's still leaking. I'll give you five thousand, but the first two month's rent will count toward the purchase price."

The realtor studied Uriah and looked at me as I was walking toward them. "Okay," he said. "Rent to buy at five thousand."

Afternoon Delight

Cass, the red-haired, freckle-faced woman we met at Andy and Sunshine's party, and Seamus, her husband, had become close friends. Cass pounded on the newly restored, pine piano we bought from Hermie just before we moved. He had a job at the new Promise Piano Company. The piano was the lone piece of furniture in the room between the kitchen and the living room of the new house. The room had no other purpose so we called it, "The Piano Room" for lack of a better description.

I flicked on the kitchen light, "Jesus!" Cockroaches scuffled in every direction back to their homes between the layers of linoleum we hadn't the time to remove. I grabbed the Rocky Road ice cream, bowls and spoons, and tip-toed across the floor to the porch.

"What were you screeching about in there?" Seamus asked.

"It was the nightly gathering of the cockroaches. I'm glad they don't eat people."

"Oh, but they do!" Alex teased, as he searched on his guitar for the chords to La Cucaracha.

"Do all of you want ice cream?"

Cass followed me to the porch. "Just a spoonful for me"

Uriah and I had invited a few people over for a house warming party. A new couple from Baton Rouge sat on the porch railing, "What a beautiful night," Johnny said, "I didn't think I would survive the winter."

Uriah laughed, "You came in April."

Johnny's partner, Amelia said, "Yeah, but it was cold in April!"

"You'll get used to it," Cass said.

The conversation drifted from the weather to Seamus using Cass as a model for his paintings. He and Cass had studied art at Murray State University in Kentucky. "Did I hear right that you have a painting hanging in a museum in Kentucky?" Amelia asked.

"He does," Cass answered, although the question hadn't been directed toward her. "He won a portrait contest."

"It's a painting of Cass," Seamus said. "She makes a great model."

"I'm a *convenient* model."

"No, you have interesting features," Seamus said.

"Should I thank him? Interesting?"

"Definitely thank him," Amelia said.

During the conversation, Alex strayed around on his guitar and made up corny songs about summer love. No one paid much attention until he began to play *Afternoon Delight*. There was an immediate protest.

I covered my ears, "God Alex, must you? What a sappy song."

Cass said, "The name of the group that sings it is just as bad— The Starland Vocal Band."

Alex continued, in spite of the protest, until I pulled his hand from the guitar. "Stop!"

After stretched out good-byes, I gathered the ice cream bowls and beer bottles. Uriah walked into the driveway with Seamus to finish a conversation about painting a mural in an Italian hair salon—the first big remodeling project of Uriah's business.

Alex followed me into the kitchen. "I hope Rita's okay," I said, "She's probably wondering why you didn't visit her tonight."

"Maybe," Alex replied, "but I've been at the hospital for days and I needed a break. The doctor said Rita's bleeding is under control and she and the baby will be able to come home in a couple of days."

"How are you feeling about the hysterectomy?"

"I think I'm okay. We've talked before about not having any more kids."

"Did having three girls give you pause on that decision?"

"Not now it doesn't."

"No, I guess not. I'm sorry, Alex, that was a dumb thing to say."

"Hey, come here," Alex reached out to me. "You couldn't say a hurtful thing if you tried."

"Not to you anyway." We embraced and rocked back and forth until we heard the cars back out of the driveway and footsteps on the porch.

"I'll see you tomorrow then?" Alex asked.

I looked at him questioningly. "Oh, to fix the stove, sure."

"I'll have the girls with me."

Good. The kids can play together."

"Look, Uriah." We stood together and brushed our teeth at the bathroom sink. "Amelia left her necklace hanging here—it's beautiful."

"She must have intended it for you."

"You think so?"

"She wouldn't have put it on the nail otherwise."

"But I hardly know her."

"She's a stained-glass artist and you're her new friend."

"Yeah, but still."

"She's beautiful too," Uriah said, raising his eyebrows at me.

I poked him with my elbow, "I suppose so." A slight twinge of jealously made me suck in a breath, but I dismissed the feeling. I took the necklace from the nail. "Look at this, Amelia pressed a Queen Anne's Lace between two pieces of glass and made a tiny glass window. I can't believe she left this for me, maybe she forgot it. I'll ask her the next time I see her."

Misfired

woke up, rolled over, and knew immediately if I moved again, I would throw up. "Oh, yuck," I said aloud.

"Are you sick?" Uriah asked, rummaging around in the dark to find clean underwear.

"I'm a little queasy. I only had one beer last night—maybe it was Johnny's gumbo. Are you getting dressed already?"

"I'm meeting Seamus and Hermie in Lockport. Seamus is going to start on the mural today."

"You want some breakfast?"

"I have to go—I'll get something later. See you."

"Wait a minute, a kiss?" I jumped up to keep him from slipping away, but had to run to the bathroom."

"You okay, Alodie?"

"I think I might be pregnant!"

"Really?"

"Yeah, maybe. Go Uriah. We'll see."

I showered and chose my clothes carefully. I decided on an Indian print skirt and a delicate blouse I had made from an embroidered curtain. I pulled the sides of my hair back, but left the rest free. Milo and Zea were tumbling about upstairs. I boiled water for oatmeal in an electric frying pan. After the kids ate, I tidied the house as well as possible. There were unpacked boxes in every room—no use unpacking when remodeling would start soon.

Alex and Rita had moved to Dwight during the winter and only lived five blocks away. He and his two girls arrived at ten o'clock. "Want some coffee?" I asked.

"Among other things."

I suddenly got the jitters. Alex wasn't wasting any time making his intentions known and I played along. I brushed a finger along his neck as I reached behind him for the coffee pot and he grabbed my hand and spun me into his arms.

"Alex, the kids."

"Let's send them to the park."

"I'll have to walk them over because the bridge is dangerous. Don't go away."

"I'll start on the stove, hurry back."

I made going to the tiny neighborhood park sound like a trip to Disneyland and the kids unanimously agreed. The covey of children followed in single file on the sidewalk and around the corner. The sidewalk ended and we stayed on the edge of the cobblestone street, then squeezed along the narrow bridge hugging tightly to the cement arches. The thicket of brambles and mulberry trees hung over the edge of the bridge on both ends—the brush limited the vision of even the most careful driver.

"Here we are," I said, as though we had walked for miles instead of the length of three city lots. "I'll come back to get you in a little while and we'll have a picnic in the back yard." I tried to leave the park without appearing to hurry, but when I reached the driveway, I ran, took two steps at a time onto the porch, and let the screen door slam.

Alex swooped me into his arms, kissed me full on the mouth and carried me into the bedroom. "You don't know how long I've been waiting for this."

We fell onto the bed, but Alex backed away. "What's wrong?"

"My gun kind of misfired."

I laughed. Even snorted. "Probably a good thing," I said.

"It's not that funny. I'm embarrassed."

I tried to hold in my laughter, got up and gave Alex a hug. "Forget about it. Let's pretend this didn't happen." We went back into the kitchen. Alex was silent while I bustled around and made the kids sandwiches.

"I'll probably tell Uriah what happened."

"Why would you tell him? Nothing really happened."

"I tell him everything—we don't keep secrets."

"That seems dumb to me."

"It isn't dumb, Alex, that's what we do."

"I want you to tell Rita, and tell her it's over, because it shouldn't have happened in the first place."

"Whatever Alodie, nothing happened."

"Something did happen! This has been brewing for months, and now you're mad."

"I'm not mad."

"You're acting mad."

"Yeah, maybe, and disappointed."

I felt dazed the rest of the afternoon—not sure how I felt. I had laughed at the time, but now I felt sorry and stupid. Really stupid.

When Uriah came home, it didn't take him long to notice my disquiet. I couldn't hold out, even though I considered not saying anything.

"Guess what happened this morning?"

"You made it with Alex."

"Not exactly. How did you know?"

"Well, you've been working up to it for months."

"Was it that obvious?"

"Yes."

I told Uriah with as little detail as possible what had happened. "Hon, I feel really sorry. I'm an idiot."

The next day passed without hearing from Alex, so did the next and the next. I began to watch for his truck to go by.

Rita called, "Hey, stranger, when are you coming over to see our new baby?"

"I didn't know if you'd be ready for a visitor."

"Alodie, get over here."

I walked downtown with the kids and carefully looked both ways at the railroad tracks that split Main Street in two. Amtrak, apparently, had made a deal with the city about speed limits and the trains flew by alarmingly fast. As we walked the last few blocks, I rehearsed what I would say to Rita about my relationship with Alex.

While admiring the new baby girl, Rita told me in detail the complications of her delivery. "I so wanted to have a natural birth, but it just wasn't going to happen and then I started bleeding—like I did the last time." She stepped back from the crib. "Oh, shit. I left the iron on. Come with me, Alodie, I want to finish the kitchen curtains so I can hang them back up."

While Rita concentrated on her work, I squirmed. "Rita? Did Alex tell you anything about what happened?" My ambiguity didn't cover the odd tone in my voice and Rita caught it instantly. She stiffened with the anger of understanding.

"That Shit!"

"Well, nothing really happened, but it could have. It was my idea too. We've been kind of sweet on each other for a long time."

"I know you were, but it makes me furious that Alex went through with it. I thought we were over that part of our lives."

"I hoped Alex would tell you."

"He never would have."

"Maybe I should stick around until he gets home. I haven't seen him since you were in the hospital and he's going to be pretty upset that I told you."

"He's coming home late and we need to straighten this out ourselves."

"You're right. I'm sorry for messing things up—you told me before there had been a problem. I let my affection cloud my judgment. We've all been so open with each other that I thought we could pull this off. Still friends?"

"Right now, I'm pissed off and I need to cool down."

The eddy of thoughts and feelings funneled down into the dark realization that as much as I wanted to redo the last few weeks, I couldn't. My biggest fear was losing our friendship with Rita and Alex.

CR

Uriah set his thermos on the kitchen table, "You're not going to believe what Alex said to me today."

"What?"

"He thinks I should have an affair with Rita to even things out."

"No way!"

"That's what I thought. Besides, I'm not attracted to her."

"Even if you were, it's weird for Alex to think that would fix things."

"The news about Victor has set Promise on edge and his behavior has given infidelity a green light. Was everyone married to someone else at Promise in their past lives?"

"That's not what happened with Alex."

"I know it wasn't." Uriah paused and looked down, "One other thing, Alodie."

"I bristled at Uriah's tone."

"What?"

"I kind of came on to Linda at the dance. You were working and I thought maybe ..."

"Did anything happen?"

"No. She told Michael and he was furious."

"Everything has gone crazy at Promise, maybe it's time to leave."

"Maybe we've left already."

Warning Sirens

"**F**inish eating your breakfast, Milo. Don't you want to see the parade?" He knew how much pleading I was capable of to get to him eat, not that he really needed the food. It was the principle of the thing—I was the mom, and he was the kid. "You're going to love the parade and it's going to come right past the house. You'll get all kinds of candy, but you must eat your granola first."

Why was he pulling this stunt today? Probably because he knew how much *I* wanted to see the July 4th bicentennial parade. "I'm going to clean the bedroom, and when I'm done, I want *you* to be done." And then what? I gave in too often and the kids knew it.

I whipped the bedspread over the pillows and picked up a pair of dirty socks Uriah had thrown at the laundry basket and missed. Picking up his dirty socks reminded me of how mad I was at him the day before. He had paneled over three beautiful Japanese prints I had hung on the stairway wall.

"I didn't know," he said. "Why didn't you take them down if you wanted to keep them?"

"I didn't know you were going to start working your way up the steps. I can't anticipate you're every move."

"They were just calendar prints, Alodie."

"You don't care whether something might be meaningful to me. Just last week you banged that piece of drywall into the mobile I made. Can't you be more careful?"

"I told you not to decorate until I'm finished."

"This place doesn't feel like home."

"It will. I'm working as fast as I can."

I was sentimental, but it still seemed like I was right—being pregnant and living in a mess wasn't a good combination.

"Here I come, Milo." He hadn't eaten a single bite. The provocation was too much. I was ready to cry. I took the bowl of soggy granola and dumped it on his head. He looked stunned for a moment, as did Zea who sat across the table. Then, they started to laugh. I tried to stay angry, but it was hopeless. I wasn't about to let this 2-1/2-year-old wreck my day.

"Come on you little squirt. Let's get you cleaned up and go see the parade."

The parade was a little longer, but hardly more spectacular than any small-town parade on any 4th of July. The kids didn't care—they loved it.

CB

At the library the next day, Milo made a beeline for the shelf on the back wall of the children's section. He knew the exact location of the bulldozer books. The librarian chuckled when he lifted his books high above his head to place them on the counter. "I see you're taking out your favorites this time, Milo." He responded with a flash of his eyes and a big smile.

In the foyer, I stopped to chat with a woman from the book club I had recently joined. Her son, maybe a year older than Milo, wore a plastic fireman's hat.

"Wow, I like your hat," I said. "Where did you get it?"

"At the fire station."

"That's exciting."

The boy's mother explained. "He goes to a great day-care. It's really more like a pre-school. The woman who runs it takes the kids on field trips every Thursday."

"What's her name?"

"Mary Mulroney."

The woman and I chatted until the boys got rowdy. "I better go," I said. "See you in a couple of weeks."

I put Milo in the bicycle seat, pedaled across town to the grocery store, and then stopped at Alex and Rita's to pick up Zea who had been playing with their girls.

"You're looking good." Alex was standing behind the open trunk of their car when I road into the driveway. "I heard from Uriah that you're going to have another baby."

I didn't reply to his comment. I just started in on him, "Are you okay, Alex? You just disappeared. What's going on?"

Alex picked up a golf bag from the ground and put it in the trunk.

"Golf? You play golf?" I barely took a breath, "What happened, Alex?"

Rita opened the porch door and Alex became edgy and slammed the trunk. "Nothing happened, Alodie. Let's forget it."

"We can still talk to each other, can't we?" I grabbed his elbow, "Come see me sometime. We should talk."

"I don't think that's a good idea."

Rita seemed perfectly at ease as we sipped our coffee. "Are you going to have your baby at home?" she asked.

"I think so. I delivered so fast with the Zea and Milo that I might not make it to the hospital anyway, but honestly, Uriah and I haven't talked much about it yet. I always meant to ask you why you didn't stay home, Rita, but I didn't want to pry."

"For the very reason I ended up with a hysterectomy. For one thing, I bleed out easily, and for another, my uterus inverted with the first delivery and it was too chancy." Rita changed the subject, "I've been thinking about going to nursing school."

"Really?"

"I love watching you during a delivery. You know so much and it's so exciting!" Rita had accompanied me a few times—an extra pair of hands really helped.

"And frightening. At least so far, there haven't been any disasters. Ever since Jane Caine started helping me with childbirth classes and telling her story the women are more accepting of going to the hospital if I think the risk is too great."

"Alex and I have been thinking of moving further north. We could still go to meetings, although we're kind of tired of Promise. I could go to school and there would be plenty of work for Alex in the Joliet area. He wouldn't have to drive as far."

"What do you mean, Rita? Are you considering dropping out?"

"We didn't think Promise would become a free for all. We love the philosophy, but Victor worship is mindless, especially after all the womanizing he did."

I felt a twinge of guilt, but Rita didn't flinch.

"Has that weirdo, Morell, come onto you? He's old enough to be my father. Out of the blue he told me about his sexual fantasies and invited me to a porn flick. Unfortunately, he lives down the street and I run into him way too often."

"I haven't met him yet. Uriah said he was implying that some of us who have been at Promise for a while are dead wood."

"What an ass. What does *he* know?"

"Another creepy idea that is swirling around Promise," I said, "is about stock piling weapons in case hungry hordes come from Chicago when the cataclysm hits."

"Oh, for Pete's sake. No one even knows we exist."

"I hate that doomsday nonsense."

"It *is* in the book."

"I know, but it's bogus. I mean, how many times in the history of the world has there been a prophecy of doom?" There was a lull in the conversation.

"I better get home. I've got a few groceries in the basket of my bike that should be put away."

I lifted Milo into his bicycle seat. Zea climbed onto the handle bars and let her legs dangle around the basket. We took a detour to visit Uriah who was covering the stained-glass windows of the Congregational church with plexiglass.

"Hi, Daddy." Both kids yelled up to Uriah who was on a ladder at the top of a window.

"Hi, kiddos. I can't come down right now."

"That's okay. We just wanted to check on you. We'll see you at home."

ೞ

Milo's new friend from across the street was in the yard when we arrived. "You guys want to play inside while I put the groceries away?" Milo and his friend went into the piano room and started wrestling—Milo called it 'bull-fighting'. It was his favorite sport.

The sky was getting dark and I checked the time. It was only four o'clock. A gust of wind shook the house. The storm warning sirens began to blow. I called to Zea, who was playing upstairs, "Come, quickly, Zea, we need to go next door." There wasn't a cellar or a basement in our house and I had made an arrangement with the neighbors to use theirs if there was a storm. I grabbed Milo and his friend by the shoulders and pushed them in front of me out the door. I could hear something banging on the roof. I looked up and saw the fiberglass sheets Uriah bought for the solar collector lifting in the wind. The material was expensive. I had to do something.

The neighbor girl was in her front yard gathering the garbage cans and toys that might blow away. "Susan, can you take my kids into your basement? I need to get up on the roof."

I heard Milo's friend's mom calling to him. "He's over here," I yelled back. I looked both ways for cars and gave him a nudge. "Hurry. Go to your mom."

Ignoring my fear of heights, I set the extension ladder against the porch roof. I climbed to the single-story addition and then hoisted myself to the second story. By this time, the fiberglass sheets had slid down and were hanging half over the edge of the roof. I was in a sitting position and scooted down as far as I dared, but I couldn't reach the fiberglass. I took a deep breath—my knees were weak and shaking. I rolled onto my belly and while fighting the wind, was able to drag the sheets along the roof, ease them down to the single story, to the porch roof, and then to the ground. I shoved the fiberglass under the open porch floor and dashed to the neighbor's under a threatening sky.

An awful smell rushed at me as I entered the house. Susan's mother, dressed in pajamas, was on the telephone in the kitchen. Barely looking up, she pointed through the dining room to the basement stairway. I picked my way over piles of dirty laundry. A quick glance into the living room revealed the source of the pervasive odor. There were soda cans and glasses half filled with water and cigarette butts on every available surface.

The power had gone out. Carefully, I felt my way down the stairs in the dim light. In the corner of the room, Zea, Milo, Susan, and her brother and sister sat on a pile of boxes. "Watch out for the dog poop," Susan said. I stopped on the bottom step.

We waited out the storm. I was worried about Uriah, but didn't say so to the kids. Susan's mom never came into the basement. When I surfaced with the kids and crossed into our own yard, I saw Uriah calmly sitting on the front porch. "You're okay?" I asked, "and the windows?"

"I'm fine. I made it home just before it got really bad. I don't know about the windows. I heard that a tornado hit the trailer court east of town." Uriah hugged me tightly, "You saved the fiberglass."

"It wasn't easy," I said, and buried my face on his chest.

Edged in Blue

Zea had been exuberant one minute, irritable the next. She was going to a *real* school. The anticipation caused emotional chaos. We had decided to send Zea to first grade at the public school. Promise was twenty miles from Dwight, too far to drive on a regular basis. On her first day of her new school, Zea woke up earlier than Uriah.

"Okay. Okay. We're up."

"No, you won't be late."

"Yes, we'll walk with you and help you find your room."

"Why don't you go upstairs and get dressed while I make breakfast." I heard a loud thud in the stairwell, then, an agonizing cry.

"What happened?"

Zea sat half way up the stairs with her arms around her knees. "I stabbed my knee."

"On what?"

"I don't know. It hurts! It's bleeding."

"Let me see, Honey." There was a puncture wound, swollen and edged in blue.

"We better find out what stabbed you." For whatever reason, Zea had crawled up the steps and had poked her knee on something hidden in the filthy rust colored shag carpet. I felt back and forth along several steps, but found nothing. "Maybe it's time to rip out this yucky carpet. Come with me to the bathroom and I'll clean up your knee. We better hurry."

Children were merging from three directions as Zea, Milo and I rounded the corner of the yellow mansion that everyone in town called, "The Lodge." We continued past the construction site of the new Methodist church and into the school parking lot. Zea squeezed my hand more and more tightly. "It's okay to be a little scared. Look at all these kids, you'll make a lot of new friends today."

A teacher stood at the first-grade classroom door. "Hello," she said. "I'm Miss Anderson. What's your name?"

"Zea."

"This is your first day at our school, isn't it?"

"Yes."

"Come with me and we'll find you a desk."

"Good-bye, Zea. I'll meet you after school." Zea barely turned to say good-bye—she was already on her way.

"Today, Buddy, we're going to see if we can talk to Mary Mulroney." Milo had been pestering Uriah and me for weeks about going to preschool. I helped him off the toilet. "You might need to go potty by yourself when you go to school." He was toilet trained but would not stand up. He needed help to get on and off the stool. He also insisted that one of us stayed with him until he was done. I thought I could try preschool as leverage for normalizing the procedure, but so far Milo wasn't going for it.

"Uriah?" I knelt on the floor and hung my head into the crawl space where he was digging, bucket by bucket, a cistern to hold the water for his trickle method solar collector. "Can I get you anything?"

A muffled, "No," came up with the smell of mold and dirt. "I found another cool bottle." A few seconds later, a muddied hand thrust a blue glass medicine bottle through a hatch cut in the floor. "Here." The house renovation had produced a trove of artifacts, including colored glass bottles, a spittoon and an old slate chalk board.

"Hon?"

"Yeah?"

I'm going to take Milo on a bike ride to Mary Mulroney's. We might stop at the park on the way home. Do you need anything from town?"

"Some money would be nice." Uriah climbed out of the pit.

"Sorry. I can't help you with that."

"I have an appointment at the other bank later today. I hope they go for the idea of a construction loan." Uriah was having trouble borrowing money for remodeling the house. He speculated the bankers didn't like the looks of the place or they were nervous about the recession, but, most likely, he was young, had no equity, and was not a local boy.

"I don't know," Mary Mulroney hesitated. My face showed instant disappointment. Milo was so determined and because it was his own idea to go to preschool, I wanted it to happen for him. He had been rather shy until now. Mary caught my expression. "He's only two and a half—I don't usually take children until they're three. Is he toilet trained?"

"Mostly. He likes to have help that he doesn't need."

Mary looked at Milo, who was already playing with trucks and another little boy. "Okay. Let's give him a try—maybe two mornings a week would be plenty at first. We'll see how he adjusts to the older kids."

"Thank you, so much, just let me know if there are any problems. When can I bring him?"

"How about next Tuesday and Thursday from nine to eleven." Mary let Milo play for a few minutes and then gave him a tour of the house. When she finished, she said, "Good-bye, Milo, nice to meet you. I'll see you next week." He stood tall and smiled.

I couldn't get Milo to come down the slide at the city park. The slide descended from the third level of an enclosure of steel bars painted red, white and blue. The bars were bent into a cage shaped like a rocket. "Milo, we have to go. We need to pick up Zea pretty soon." I debated trying to squeeze through the child size openings to the top platform to fetch him, but instead hopped on the bike and made like I was going home. He knew I wouldn't leave him, but felt my seriousness and came down.

Uriah picked up Zea from school on his way home from the bank. They were talking cheerfully as they entered the house—Zea about school and Uriah about financial relief.

ও৪

The following week an early frost had turned the trees in the neighborhood multiple shades of red, yellow and orange. Leaves were piling up in the yard and while Zea and Milo were at school, I raked them into piles for them to play in when they got home. The repetitive movement, the crisp air and the smell of the fallen leaves caught me up in a reverie until a car peeled through the intersection and over the bridge. There was an immediate sickening sound of an impact and the squeal of brakes.

I dropped the rake and ran around the neighbor's house. I could see a red tricycle as I ascended the rise of the bridge, and then I saw a child lying in the middle of the street. A teenage boy paced around a Chevy Malibu half a block ahead. I shouted to him, "Go to that house and call an ambulance!" A little boy, three, maybe four years old, was stretched out on the pavement, white as death. I checked his pulse—strong. He was breathing irregularly, gurgling. I checked his pupils—unequal, markedly so. I could see he had hit the back of his head. He didn't move. I called to him, but he didn't respond.

The boy's mother came out of her house and panicked when she saw her son. The teenager came out of a brick house and I ordered the mother, "Find out if that kid called an ambulance." I noticed the little boy's lips were edged in blue—he wasn't getting enough air. In case his breathing stopped altogether, I got into position to start CPR. Then I heard the ambulance siren.

An EMT asked me the usual questions and immediately said, "His airway must be obstructed." A second EMT stabilized the boy's neck and swept his throat. Nothing. Three quick abdominal thrusts dislodged a big wad of purple gum. The boy began to breathe more easily, his color improved, but he didn't regain consciousness. The ambulance screamed away.

I answered a few questions barked at me by a greasy-haired policeman and went home. I sat on the front porch while my adrenaline rush gradually subsided. I was mortified that I hadn't checked the boy's airway. I berated myself over and over. *What was I thinking? Incompetent. I was incompetent.*

When Uriah came home, I told him the story, every detail. "I feel so stupid."

"Alodie, come on. Look at everything you did. You probably saved the boy's life."

As the evening hours came, so did forgiveness. I did after all, rush quickly to the scene. I called for help. I checked the boy's pulse and breathing—initially. I knew he wasn't breathing effectively. I assessed his pupils and warned of a neck and head injury. I helped the mother focus by giving her a task, but I missed an important detail, which I would have noticed immediately if I had given the boy a breath.

I fell asleep with the thought that I probably had saved the boy's life, and I knew I would never, ever, make the same mistake again.

Am I Right?

lay huddled under as many blankets as we had. Before I fell asleep, I used a fetal scope to listen to the baby's heartbeat. The rate was one-hundred forty quick strong beats a minute. I couldn't guess the baby's sex. The heart rate was smack in the middle between that of a boy or a girl. I had been a little queasy at first, but not puking sick like I had been with Milo. He had been carried low and deep—this baby was high and in front, but not as high as Zea.

When I left work an hour before, the temperature on the bank read twenty-five below zero. I was glad the car started, but the heater couldn't outdo the cold. Uriah took the kids to Herman and Georgia's for a while, so I could sleep. I didn't think it was a good idea, but Uriah had insisted, and I needed sleep. The wind was blowing snow across the roads from the day before and more snow was to come, although it seemed too cold for snow.

I tried to unwind and warm up. I usually used the time in the car to settle down after a busy night, but the cold and drifting had kept my mind on task. My heart ached for a co-worker whose baby was born six weeks earlier with the umbilical cord wrapped twice tightly around its neck. The baby didn't breathe for several minutes and needed to be resuscitated. He was initially flown to the Champaign/Urbana neonatal unit and had returned to the pediatric unit in Kankakee until arrangements could be made for him to be cared for at home. I had taken care of the baby that night and couldn't get the blank stare and the flaccid body out of my mind. I decided I couldn't float to pediatrics again while I was pregnant or had little kids—it was too worrisome.

I couldn't warm up. We had moved upstairs while Uriah worked on the first floor. The house was incredibly drafty and central heat was still a dream. The current source of heat was a natural gas space heater in the piano room. It was barely able to keep the room at fifty degrees, let alone warm the rest of the house. A little heat drifted up the steps, so the warmest area was at the top of the stairs where the bed had been temporarily placed.

I watched the light reflecting on tiny particles of snow that blew through the cracks around the window sash. I began to shiver on a trip to the bathroom and by the time I huddled under the blankets again, I was shaking uncontrollably. "I have never been this cold in my entire life!" I yelled, as I beat my legs and arms against the mattress until I got over the chills and fell asleep.

A scramble of feet on the steps woke me up seconds before I was pummeled by knobby elbows and knees. "We were stuck, Mom!" Zea tugged at her knotted scarf.

"Oh, yeah?" I sat up.

"We had to walk through drifts—really far."

I pulled Zea close to look at her face. "You have a white spot on your nose, Honey."

"My nose was really cold."

Uriah came into the room. "I got stuck in a drift about a half mile from Herman's. We had to walk. It was really stupid to go out there."

'You didn't know the drifts would be that deep."

"I could have guessed. I just kept trying to ram through."

"What happened?"

"The plow came by and Herman helped me dig the car out. It wasn't too bad."

"I'll get up and make some spaghetti. We can have a picnic in bed, if you guys will be careful."

Uriah finished the last of his food and said, "Herman and Georgia are leaving Promise, they're moving to California in the spring."

"Oh, no. Why?"

"They think it was a mistake to come to Promise in the first place and they're tired of the politics. Hermie's growing out his mustache."

"Do he and Georgia know what they'll do in California?"

"I don't know about Georgia, but Hermie wants to start his own piano restoration business. Do you think we made a mistake by coming to Promise?"

"I don't know, I think it's been good for us."

"I'm sure going to miss them."

"Yeah, me too."

The squawking crunch of a crowbar became the squeak of a door in my dream. Another early morning of construction. Uriah had pulled the walls apart to fix the bathroom and turn a bedroom into a new kitchen. "It's going to be a mess for a while," he said. I shrugged. I had resigned myself to dust and debris until the day the house was finished, but we would be lucky to live in it shiny new for more than a week or two. The plan was to sell it as soon possible.

The smell of mold, decaying creatures and rotting wood, and the sound of a sledge hammer, a crowbar and a skill saw filled my waking hours. "This poor baby is going to be a nervous wreck!" I shouted to Uriah as he cut though an original stud wall, blackened with age.

As he pried a two by four from the grip of its square nails, a box fell to the floor. "Alodie, look at this." A faded Christmas card box tied with yellowed string had been hidden on a cross brace in the wall. Uriah shook it, "Sounds like a button box." He cut the string with his utility knife. "Seeds." He handed me the box.

"What kind are they?"

"You're asking me?" Uriah started the saw.

"Some kind of flower seeds," I yelled. "I wonder how old they are? Do you think they'll grow?" Uriah pointed to his ear—unable to hear me.

I was excited about the seeds. There was something deeply nostalgic they triggered in me. I would plant them along the front of the house and along the west side of the Quonset shed.

CR

"I don't believe in evil," I said emphatically at a book club meeting in late winter. "It's overrated and the idea makes people crazy. I was raised in a church where the preacher harped constantly about evil. He made me feel guilty for not feeling guilty. Why not concentrate on the good in people?"

"How can you NOT believe in evil?" the Nazarene minister's wife predictably countered, "It's scriptural."

A look of giddy anticipation crossed the face of my new friend, Bronte. "What do you mean, Alodie?" She knew very well what I meant, but I took the bait.

"In my experience, a refusal to admit mistakes, a lack of honest communication and a relentless refusal to forgive make the world less than perfect, but the Devil did not make me do anything." I thrived on book club discussions. Promise had given me so many new ways of thinking about the world. The caffeine overload carried all of us easily past midnight. I continued without a breath so no one else could get a word in. "And then there is bad karma— the dumb stuff you did in one life, that if you don't fix, follows you into the next."

We were buzzed. One intriguing theme shaped-shifted to another and another until the real world of work and kids nudged us home one by one.

Bronte's cowboy boots clicked along the sidewalk as we walked the four blocks home. Bronte was still in overdrive, rehashing and reliving the highlights of the evening. "Come over tomorrow and keep me company for a while," I said, jaywalking across the intersection of our departure. "I need to putter around and do some laundry and cleaning. It's Milo's preschool day.

Bronte and I had met as spectators on the bleachers of the high school football field during the town's Halloween costume parade. Bronte wasn't her given name— changing it from Nancy fit with her other eccentricities. Her dark, waist-long hair, skin tight blue jeans and cowboy boots accentuated her lankiness.

I envied Bronte's creativity even more than I envied Uriah's. He could draw and build anything and play any instrument. Bronte had studied weaving in college. I didn't know that was possible. She designed quilts, sewed clothes without using patterns, had made a host of papier-mâché creatures, and was teaching herself to play the slide-guitar. With no kids to slow her down, and a husband that supported her for the time being, Bronte was free to do as she pleased. She and Uriah had hit it off; she loved to hear his latest scheme.

A knock on the door the next morning proved not to be Bronte. An over-sized man in an over-sized suit jacket made a show of his preacher-sized Bible. "Nice day, am I right?" he asked.

Darn. I thought. Still feeling a hangover of confrontation from the book club discussion, I decided to take him on.

"I noticed you've been working on your house, am I right?"

Obviously

"I wanted to invite you to our church, if you're not already attending."

"I don't go to church." I held the door open. "Would you like a cup of coffee?" I clearly had the edge and the preacher hesitated to come into my lair. I let him squirm, but he followed me into the kitchen.

"Do you believe in Jesus as your personal savior?"

"No."

The preacher began to twitch. "But we all need to be saved."

"From what?"

"From sin and temptation—from going to hell."

"I don't believe in that." I put two cups on the table and motioned for him to sit.

"What do you mean, you don't believe in that?"

"I think it's all a lot of nonsense—a big scam to control people and keep them from discovering their own spirituality."

"How can you say that? If the word of God isn't the truth, I just spent three years in seminary for nothing, am I right?" The preacher inched backwards toward the kitchen door.

I was dumbfounded by that statement. His waste of three years was his biggest concern? What about my soul?

I couldn't help a hint of a smile. "Yeah, hmm, you're probably right."

The preacher had enough of me and was losing any semblance of righteous calm. "Well, I'm sorry for you." He opened the door and stepped outside.

"Thanks for coming," I said.

Disconnected

noticed the tulips had poked their sword-like leaves into the air along the south side of the house, and I suspended painting the table for a moment. It was the first day of March, spring had come early and I let the sun warm my face. The legs of the enamel topped table were getting their yearly makeover as part of my nesting flurry. Uriah was inside disconnecting the remaining framework of the abandoned kitchen from the rest of the house.

"I'll wait for Zea to get home from school to pull the kitchen off," he said during lunch. "She and the neighbor kids might like to watch."

"No doubt," I said. We sat in the new kitchen. The soft golden yellow walls and pine cabinets gave the room a sunset glow. The floor was covered with cloth that Uriah had cut into triangles, arranged in a quilt-like pattern and then varnished with polyurethane. The floor made the room feel cozy—a charming place to finish our meal.

The sputtering of an engine next door grew louder and deeper.

"You've got to be kidding," Uriah said, as he pulled back the eyelet curtains. "Sam started his steam engine."

"In the driveway? I thought he'd take the thing to the country to tinker on it."

"Guess not."

Sam's driveway was only a few feet from the north side of the house. The possibility of noise from a steam engine wasn't taken into account in the middle of the winter when the placement and remodeling of the kitchen was planned and carried out.

"Do you think he'll keep that racket up all summer?"

"There must be an ordinance against it."

"You think so? Against a steam engine?"

"Against making that much noise."

"Let's hope so."

"I'll talk to Sam about it before I complain. Maybe this is a one-time trial."

Uriah hooked a chain from the corner post of the old kitchen to the axle of the pickup. "Everybody ready? Stand back a little bit more, okay? I don't know exactly what's going to happen." He revved the engine of the truck and pulled his foot from the clutch. It sputtered and died. He tried again, a little more slowly. With the wheels spinning and the clutch burning, the kitchen separated and broke apart in an explosion of dust and crashed to the ground. A cheer went up from the spectators.

"That memory will keep for a lifetime," I said.

"It was pretty cool, wasn't it?"

"Very cool."

I was uncomfortable. For the last six weeks, I hadn't been able to roll over in bed. I had to stand up to lie down on my other side. I had forgotten the feel of a full night's rest. At nine-thirty in the evening an unusual twinge in my lower abdomen sent me quickly to the bathroom. Bloody show and amniotic fluid—the time had come.

I called the hospital in Kankakee where Uriah had taken a temporary part-time job on the mental health unit during the winter construction slowdown.

"Are you sure it's time?"

"Of course. Come home as soon as you can. Drive safely, though."

Georgia and Amelia would drive together and arrive within forty-five minutes. I had asked Georgia to help me because she was always calm and had the experience of birthing her own kids. I had grown to love Amelia; she was kind and intuitive and her presence was reassuring. Lastly, I called the EMT who had been on the scene of the accident by the bridge. I ran into him a few times afterward, and asked, not that he attend the birth, but to stand by in case I needed to be rushed to the hospital.

I didn't call Rita. She and Alex had recently moved to Joliet. The distance was a factor, but also, it just didn't feel right. Perhaps she would want to take control, or maybe she felt some lingering resentment—maybe not, but I went with my gut.

The supplies were in order, waiting in the closet. Contractions were regular at three minutes apart by the time everyone arrived.

The birth would take place in the living room. The bed had been moved again to another temporary spot, the last time before it was moved into the back room which would then become the master bedroom. Comforting forest green walls, cream trim and a mottled short-shag carpet adorned the newly finished living room.

"Are you going to wake up the kids pretty soon?" Amelia wondered, as I rocked back and forth with forearms on the kitchen table. I held one finger up to my lips to signal a delay in my response.

"I'm thinking it's not such a good idea to have the kids watch. What do you think, Hon?" I didn't wait for a reply, "I don't want them to worry or get scared."

"You're right. We'll need to pay attention to what we're doing. Let's get them up after the baby is born."

"Another one!" I focused my attention on my breathing pattern. "This labor's taking longer than with Zea or Milo, but the contractions don't seem as painful and there's more time in between them."

I walked between rooms while Amelia, Georgia and Uriah wondered about the baby's gender. "What do you think it is, Alodie?" Georgia asked.

"I still can't say. It's funny, I'm usually quite sure—and almost always right when I'm the midwife, but I just can't get a feel for this little one."

A really strong contraction began and I shouted at Uriah, "Push on my back!" He didn't delay. He had provided counter pressure to my lower back during both previous deliveries and it helped tremendously. At three o'clock, I had to lie down. "It won't be long now. I can feel the baby's head coming down." Within ten minutes the urge to push consumed me. The contractions were still around two minutes apart, which gave me time to rest and give Uriah minute by minute instructions and reassurance.

A mystical tranquility settled over me during one of these breaks. "She's here. The baby's a girl. Can you feel her?"

"I do!" Amelia replied, "It's so strong."

One of the teachings of Promise was that the soul, although it checked in on its unborn body now and then, entered the body for good immediately before or at the time of birth. I felt this to be true from my experience assisting at multiple deliveries, but I had never felt it with such a complete knowing.

"Uriah. Get ready. Can you see the head?"

He peeked under the sheet. In dismay, he cried, "It's not the head!"

"Yes, it is, I can feel it," I grunted as I pushed.

"It's all wrinkled."

"Put your hand on the head and resist just slightly so she can come out slowly." I eased up on the next push and the head came out. "Check if the cord is around the neck."

"It is!"

"Put your fingers under it and roll it over the baby's head."

Uriah did as he was told. "It fell apart! It must have been mucous."

"Good." In an instant, Aura Lee slid into the world. Uriah picked up the baby, he was speechless. He put the baby on my shrunken belly. "Look at her, Hon, she looks like your dad. Aura Lee's little forehead was compressed over her nose, giving her the appearance of an old man. "Her hair is red, isn't it?"

Aura Lee cried just a little—eyes wide open. Uriah cut and clamped the cord while I nursed the baby for the first time. We were so enamored with our new little daughter that I didn't pay attention to the contraction signaling the detachment of the placenta. After several minutes I thought aloud, "I wonder why the placenta isn't coming? Uriah, pull gently on the umbilical cord." There was no movement. If I had been able, I would have manipulated the uterus and pulled at the same time, but I couldn't instruct Uriah to do this sensitive procedure. I feared, if the placenta had not detached, I might hemorrhage if he pulled too hard.

I checked the involution of my uterus by compressing the top of it through my belly. It was clamped down hard, as it should be. "I've never had this happen. I suppose I missed my chance and now my uterus is shrinking back to normal over the placenta." I got out of bed and squatted and kneeled and pushed in every conceivable way. "It's stuck and I'll have to go to the ER and have the doctor pull it out. What a bummer!"

"Should we get the kids up before we go?" Uriah asked.

"Let's, and how about some breakfast too," I said, "I'm starving."

Georgia and Amelia stayed with Milo and Zea while Uriah, Aura Lee and I went to the hospital. "I'll try to stay positive about this— I wanted to have the baby checked over in a couple of days anyway."

At the hospital, I explained to a doctor what happened after the birth and ended with my hypothesis. "There's no evidence of bleeding and my uterus is firm, too firm, that's why the placenta won't come out—it's trapped."

The doctor, in condescending disregard of my theory, insisted on his own, "There's a chance the placenta is still attached and will need to be removed surgically."

"Can't you just try to use controlled cord traction? Something less complicated?" I was pleading now, thinking of the hospital bill we had hoped to avoid.

"I can't risk it," the doctor wouldn't budge.

I had no choice. We had decided to have the baby at home for several reasons, not just to save money. I had learned from having two kids and from my practice as a midwife that birth was a spiritual process—a deeply rich and important part of life. I didn't want strangers to interfere. We had our beautiful baby at home, but this was definitely anticlimactic.

"When did you eat last?" the anesthesiologist asked. I cringed, knowing that because of the chili omelet, I would have to wait several hours.

"We'll schedule you for one-thirty."

I nursed the baby again. "Hon, you might as well take her home. She, at least, is fine. The nurses won't allow Aura Lee in the nursery because she might have been contaminated from being born at home. I told them to put me on the medical ward, but they won't do that either because they're afraid the nurses on that unit won't know how to assess me. This whole thing stinks." I tried not to cry.

"Don't worry, Hon. I'll get the baby settled at home. Amelia or Georgia will probably be able to stay and I'll be back here around one o'clock."

"I hope she doesn't get too hungry, but she should sleep for a while now."

I decided to use the time while I waited to get a nap. I tried to relax, but I couldn't because try as I might, I couldn't urinate and my bladder became more and more distended. I knew the pressure of my uterus and the placenta was interfering. Every trick I had used on my own patients was not working on me. By ten o'clock, I begged the nurses to do something. "I need to be catheterized," I insisted. "If I don't go pretty soon, my bladder will push the uterus up and it won't be able to clamp down. Then, I *will* start bleeding."

"I'll have to get an order," the nurse replied.

"So, get one. Don't you have a standing order? Why don't you check?" I knew the nurses were perturbed, not only at my insistence, but at my perceived negligence for having a baby at home. They stalled and I was losing my patience. I rang again for a nurse, but none came. Finally, I got up, marched to the nurses' station, and yelled, "Will someone give me a catheter so I can take care of myself?!" A doctor in the dictation room heard me shout and came to the counter.

"Can I help you?"

I quickly explained the situation and he signaled to the nurse, who responded by feigning concern and hurried to my aide.

I awoke in the recovery room at one-thirty. A nurse leaned over me and smiled. "That was the quickest in and out I've ever seen. All the doc did was push on your uterus and pull on the cord. The placenta came right out."

"Exactly. Get me out of here."

On the drive home we relived Aura Lee's delivery. "Alodie, you were amazing."

Uriah's cheerfulness soothed my disappointment. "You were pretty amazing yourself. You delivered your own daughter; I'm so proud of you. What an experience!"

"It was wonderful."

Remarkable Endurance

"**G**et this, Alodie. A preacher stopped by this morning and asked me to do a couple of fix-up projects at his church. He might also have been asking if I had any work for him, but he was vague."

"He wasn't the obnoxious guy who tried to convert me, was he?"

"No, this is a young man, new to town. He noticed I was building a greenhouse above the garage and wondered if I wanted any bat guano. He said it was inches thick in the attic and belfry of his church.

"Why would we want his bat shit?"

"It used to be harvested by the ton from the Carlsbad Cavern for fertilizer."

"Is he going to bring it over or do we have to get it ourselves?"

"He'll get his people to dig it out and bring it over."

"How generous of him. Sure."

Joining the piano room to the garage, where the old kitchen had been, Uriah built a screened-in breezeway. The south slant of the garage roof was covered with clear fiberglass; the plan was to use five-gallon plastic buckets which were left over from paint and joint compound as planters. Hauling the dirt up the ladder would be a chore, but it would only have to be done once. The bat guano was a good idea, fresh manure wasn't easy to find.

Later that day, I called into the garage where Uriah was working. "I'm going for a run, is Milo with you?"

"He is."

"Aura Lee is sleeping and I'll leave the door open so you can hear her. Zea wants to run with me."

I had resumed jogging as soon as I could after Aura Lee was born. At first, I could run only two or three blocks without becoming uselessly winded, but now I was able to run two or three miles. Zea had bicycled beside me several times but had recently been asking to run with me. I tried to dissuade her because the distance seemed too long for a seven-year-old. "I'll go right home if I get tired," Zea promised, "I know the way back."

Zea pranced along with me, first two blocks, then three, then four, then five. She jabbered merrily without any sign of distress.

"Maybe we should walk a little bit. How are you doing, Zea?" The walk was clearly for my benefit.

"This is fun, Mom."

"Aren't you tired?"

"Nope, are you?"

"Yes, I'm pooped. I think you're a natural, Honey. You have remarkable endurance and can run with me anytime."

As I dragged myself up the steps into the breezeway, I saw Milo, in my peripheral vision, slide down the last few rungs of the ladder that leaned into the greenhouse. He landed on his feet and with a ferocious look on his face kicked the bottom rung. "You stupid ladder!" he scolded, and then started to cry.

Uriah quickly approached from the garage. "Milo, I told you to wait until I could help you."

I looked Milo over carefully, "You seem all right, Buddy, do you hurt anywhere?"

"That's a stupid ladder."

"Yeah, really dumb," Uriah agreed seriously. We smiled at each other without Milo noticing.

"I'm hungry, Mom," Zea said.

"I'll bet you are, I'll start supper. Aura Lee was stirring and wasn't about to wait to be fed. I nursed her football style while I cooked.

"The kids are asleep, Uriah. I'm going to take a shower. I hope you didn't notice how disgustingly smelly I am." I pulled clean pajamas from the dresser.

He grabbed my arm as I passed him. "I love the way you smell."

"Oh, sure you do, you haven't been down-wind."

"Come here, let me smell." Uriah pulled me on top of him into the bed which was now in its permanent home in the back room.

"No way. Stay awake for fifteen minutes and I'll smell like a rose."

"And you'll let me smell you then?"

"If you're good."

"We should be home around ten o'clock, Susan. The kids are fed, but there is food in the fridge for a bedtime snack. Here is a phone number if you need us. Zea and Milo, you listen to Susan, okay?"

"So, this is it," Uriah said as he started the car. "The night the verdict is announced."

By now, everyone at Promise knew of Victor's transgressions. His imprudent deeds were affirmed by women angered by his audacity and their own gullibility. "I still can't believe Victor used Promise money to have women train as masseuses and then conned them into doing him special favors. How ridiculous—it sounds like a low budget film."

"But you can't beat his line—the guy is a genius of seduction." Uriah impersonated Victor's sleazy voice, "*Oh, my darling, you were once my queen—my soul mate in a past life. Don't you remember?*"

The people of Promise decided Victor should be judged by a randomly selected group of members. Despite their fractured faith, some people still wanted Victor to stay, he was after all, the only direct link to the Brotherhood.

The meeting was brief. William, now the president, said simply, "Based on the evidence confirming Victor's deceit, and on his disregard for the laws by which we have chosen to live, the panel has decided he is no longer a member of Promise."

There was a finality to the decision that made me sad. The community would probably continue in some form, but it felt like the spark, the enthusiasm, had drained out of people. Uriah and I had become better people by practicing the Virtues and living by the Universal Laws. We had blended our childhood values with those of Promise. We had grown up and become pragmatic and self-reliant.

Our friends had moved on and there was nothing holding us to Promise. Rita and Alex were settled in Joliet; Herman and Georgia had moved to California; Seamus and Cass had moved back east, and Bronte was planning to move to Oregon.

"I wonder how Jen and Lee are doing?" Uriah mused as he poured our morning coffee.

"We haven't seen them since Aura Lee was born. I wish I had asked Jen to help us with the delivery. She didn't seem very keen on homebirth and the distance was a factor, but still, I should have asked her." Aura Lee was lifting her hands over her head and blowing bubbles to try to get our attention. "What are you doing little girl?" She made a silly face much to Zea and Milo's delight and they egged her on.

"So big." I tried to get Aura Lee to lift her arms again, and of course she wouldn't do it on command, but as soon as I gave up, she shot her hands into the air and squealed.

"What a little ham you are!" Uriah said, and kissed her forehead. His scratchy new beard tickled and she squealed again and pushed him away.

The phone rang. "Hello, Darlin' to you. I can't believe it. We were just talking about you five minutes ago … That's great!" I turned to Uriah, I couldn't wait to tell him, "Jen and Lee are going to have a baby!"

That evening, with Milo thrown over his shoulder, Uriah, Zea and I climbed the stairs to the newly finished bedrooms. Uriah had tried to be efficient with time and money and had used paneling to cover the severely cracked and broken plaster. He didn't particularly like paneling, so he made the room and the project more interesting by putting it on the walls every which way—horizontally, vertically, and diagonally. To match the paneling, he placed the new striped carpet in several directions. "It's the first night in your own room, Zea, and such an interesting room it is. You're getting to be such a grown-up little girl." After I sang her favorite bedtime lullaby from Mary Poppins and fought Milo for a hug, I said, "Good-night chickadee lambkins. Sleep tight, don't let the bed bugs bite." It was our usual routine. I put Aura Lee down in the big plywood cradle that now had beautifully painted names and birthdates on three sides.

Uriah and I sat on the front porch with our feet on the railing. The smell of four o'clocks and orange cosmos drifted up from the narrow garden along the wall of the house. These were the flowers that grew from the seeds found in the old kitchen wall. "Hon, what are we going to do after we sell the house?"

"What do you want to do, Alodie?"

"Start a new adventure, maybe move some place wild."

We heard footsteps. "We're out here." Uriah opened the door for Zea and cuddled her on his lap.

"I want to sleep in Milo's room."

"Rather than your own?"

"Yes."

"Should we make your room the playroom, like it was before?"

Zea nodded. She looked disappointed—perhaps she didn't want to feel the way she did.

"It's all right, Honey, you're used to sleeping in the same room as Milo. Come on, we'll make a place for you on the floor next to him and tomorrow morning we'll move your bed. Okay?"

When I returned to the porch, Uriah continued the conversation where we left off. "You've always wanted to live in Montana."

"It's beautiful there. I'd like to work again—maybe we should live near a city. But I would *love* to live in the mountains."

"I have an idea—why don't I blindfold you? We'll open the atlas to Montana and I'll spin you around. Wherever your finger lands, that's where we'll go."

"Really, just like that?"

"Sure, why not?"

Acknowledgements

Thanks to Tom Driscoll, Managing editor of Shipwreckt Books Publishing Company, for accepting the manuscript. He once told me proofreading was a writer's burden. For slogging through several drafts of Uriah's Utopia, and for his attention to detail, I owe my husband, Jim, my undying attention (his request). My daughter, Eliza, gave me tips on writing style and cleared up confusing passages—thanks.

There are many friends who appear fictitiously in the novel. I hope I portrayed them respectfully. Thanks to Genova Singleton, whose special gifts gave joy and wonder to the story.

Thank you to Mary Smit and Jeanette Wierman—our mothers. I hope our adventures didn't cause you to worry—too much.

About the Author

Flannery O'Connor said, "Writing is a terrible experience, during which the hair falls out and the teeth decay." Gloria Smit agrees. So, to keep a bit of hair and a few teeth, she limits her reflections and her writing to the homebound days of winter. During the warmer days of summer, Gloria putters away the hours in her gardens and greenhouse. She cares for her Icelandic sheep, walks her dog and pets her cats. Gloria and her husband, Jim, live in Wisconsin on the bluffs above the Mississippi River.

Reluctantly Exposed, Gloria's first book of autobiographical fiction, is available at www.shipwrecktbooks.press, and on Amazon.

www.ingramcontent.com/pod-product-compliance
Lightning Source LLC
Chambersburg PA
CBHW071440260626
47170CB00008B/2777